THE YOUNG AND EVIL

by

CHARLES FORD

and

PARKER TYLER

AYER COMPANY, PUBLISHERS, INC.
SALEM, NEW HAMPSHIRE 03079

The publisher wishes to thank

RICHARD BANKS

for his motivating influence

in the creation of this series

Reprints Edition, 1993
Ayer Company, Publishers, Inc.
Salem, New Hampshire   03079

Reprinted from a copy in
  The New York Public Library

HOMOSEXUALITY: Lesbians and Gay Men in
Society, History and Literature
ISBN for complete set: 0-405-07348-8
See last pages of this volume for titles.

Manufactured in the United States of America

———◆———

Library of Congress Cataloging in Publication Data

Ford, Charles Henri.
  The young and evil.

  (Homosexuality)
  Reprint of the 1933 ed. published by the Obelisk
Press, Paris.
  I. Tyler, Parker, joint author. II. Title.
III. Series.
PZ4.F6926Yo10 [PS3511.0392]   813'.5'2   75-12351
ISBN 0-405-07392-5

THE YOUNG AND EVIL

THE YOUNG AND EVIL

by

CHARLES FORD

and

PARKER TYLER

THE OBELISK PRESS
338, RUE SAINT-HONORÉ, PARIS

FIRST PRINTED 1933.
A special edition of 50 numbered
copies on pure linen Lafuma,
signed by the authors, constitutes
the original edition.

FROM C. F. TO K. T. Y.

AND

FROM P. T. TO THE MOST INTIMATE GUEST

CONTENTS

CHAPTER ONE: WELL SAID THE WOLF

WELL said the wolf to Little Red Riding Hood no sooner was Karel seated in the Round Table than the impossible happened. There before him stood a fairy prince and one of those mythological creatures known as Lesbians. Won't you join our table? they said in sweet chorus.

When he went over with them he saw the most delightful little tea-pot and a lot of smiling happy faces.

A little girl with hair over one ear got up close and said I hope you won't be offended but why *don't* you dress in girls' clothes?

The Lesbian said yes your face is so exquisite we thought you were a Lesbian in drag when we first saw you and for two long hours they insisted that he would do better for himself as a girl.

He must have fallen asleep for he awoke with a start and saw a nice fat old bullfrog beckoning to him. He went over to see what he wanted and he had a fresh cup of tea to offer Karel. Now you must recite that poem *Dreams Die Downward* that you recited at my table last time he said and what should Karel find himself doing but repeating an old nursery rhyme he learned as a child.

Then the naiads cooed with joy but at this moment he became aware that his Brooklyn Soso Flower was present with a girl and looking wistfully at him. All at once he heard a shout: Hurrah! Let's go for a boatride and the voices of the little boys and girls rang so enchantingly on the morning air that he was compelled to join them and saying good-bye hurriedly to all he left.

When they had enjoyed a splendid ride they landed at the Doll's House which is a quaint place and as he was wondering when the dreadful babble was going to end (since no one had any tea) who should walk in but Karel's nice old bullfrog himself followed by the naiads and a satyr and they signalled to Karel to come over. Almost the satyr's first words were how much do you want for a copy of that poem and Karel said he guessed two dollars and so he wrote it out. The satyr handed him two dollars which Karel folded carefully and stuck inside his bodice (when no one was looking of course) and eventually some of the party began to leave. Karel made preparations to depart likewise and waited a little while to decide what to do with such a *nice* afternoon and some men friends coming there he thought he might as well go back to the Round Table and being about to leave the fairy prince who had a watchful guardian (it may have been his elder brother) said to Karel privately we're staying at the Pennsylvania until Tuesday—do come up which almost made Karel blush. He was afraid he had drunk too much tea.

But good-bye he called and hopped off in a lovely little speedboat for the Round Table. When he got there whom should he catch sight of but a couple of old friends and one whom Karel's mother had always told him not to associate with because he was a 'sissy' asked him out to a private tea-party and Karel said yes thank you hardly knowing what he did.

But Soso Flower was beside him and even when Harold came up and began calling Karel names for not coming to see him when he *has* no telephone Karel kept back the tears because he thought of mother and suddenly the Big Black Bear who owned the cafeteria roared that it was closing and Karel thought that Harold almost had words with someone and Karel completely forgot about his promise to go on the private tea-party. He made his way as best he could through the jostling crowd followed by Harold and Soso Flower.

When the good fresh late afternoon air—the sun was a great red ball—hit them some horrid ogre accosted Karel frightening him out of his wits and without more ado about a *questionable place of entertainment* Karel gathered his hips and fled with his companions to a haven—a private home—where they ate sandwiches and drank coffee instead of tea.

CHAPTER TWO: JULIAN AND KAREL

JULIAN raised his big blue eyes from the telephone directory on the slanting shelf outside the booth on pier 36 and saw a slightly orange face containing eyes with holes in them. He had descended the gangplank of the ship from New Orleans to New York behind a Canadian that limped.

He knew that this was Karel. For one thing he expected eyelashes made up with mascara. Oh he said hello and put his hand in Karel's hand.

Karel was like a tall curved building only much smaller. He was wearing a dark green, the color of the rings around the holes, hat with an upward sweep on the left side. His overcoat seemed to fit him desperately.

Julian had shorter hair and lush expectancy. I must get my bag he said. Good-bye Mr. Canadian I hope your limp will soon disappear, no I don't want to meet your sister. When he came back to Karel they walking made so many twin posts to Eleventh Street. They went past the goal of each lamp and the shapes of men which were half-endured.

You were behind time Karel said.

Yes Julian said even the lights were more retrogressive than I.

You look as real as death Karel said.

They entered a plain hotel and walked up to the desk.

With bath? the clerk asked peering at their signatures.

Without said Julian. He saw Karel with attachment and wonder and Karel looked at him exploringly.

The room was in the best order of another decade. Julian loosened his collar and Karel arranged his long black hair. Karel had written that he used makeup achingly but unobtrusively. His eyebrows though Julian thought might cause an Italian laborer to turn completely around. They lit cigarettes.

You are the Karel who wrote me letters on nice long rotten sheets of paper Julian said. You made words on it that meant o sweet tight boy being in New Orleans *they* are the first madness of the age besides that which exists between an arctic bird's tongue and its beak. Order some gin he said.

Karel said shall I read you a poem.

Julian said yes order some gin and gingerale.

Karel folded the poem and called a number and asked for Frank. He'll be up.

Do read me your poem *Directions*.

I said in their faces the other night—*Directions*

not *Persuasions*. But then stars are the reasons for men-bewildered words.

The chandelier was uglier than either of their faces so neither looked at it.

There he is already.

Hello Frank.

Julian liked his cap.

Here you are.

Thank you.

Now ring for some ice and ask the bell-boy if he thinks art has disappeared as it's been rumored.

The bell-boy said yes sir thank you sir.

This is good gin Julian said pouring the two tumblers again half full, pouring again two half full, pouring half full again two, being used to corn whisky.

You know Jesus came to see me in Cinderella's slippers last night Karel said. Life is a dream the body should be perfumed.

Those Arabian Nights' heroes knew their stuff said Julian.

The world is growing younger over these flowers of concrete, what can one do but love Paris.

The be-poeted courtesan.

And what though I never cared for diamonds I like pink-shaded boudoir lights.

And some thighs I can remember not having known but were known Julian said on a night like a velvet Woolworth pansy sporting a stamen moon, a little lemonish thing.

Karel was wondering how a street with an elevated track over it can frame some people so well or not so well.

Julian said I think I like Djuna Barnes which is a good way to think.

Karel crossed his legs and forearms with the glass in his left hand. Yes and if Miss Barnes were to come past my gate I'd say come into my yard Miss Barnes and sit upon my porch and I will serve you tea and if you will recite one of your poems I will be glad to learn it backwards.

Julian said all things of course are going backwards past her ear.

But that is not my affair is it? Tell me how southerners look now. Until I saw you I believed they were extinct.

Not at all but the sky is different down there. In summer they peel something from it in huge slabs and nail it on you and call it the heat. I floundered in the sleek mirrors.

Would it have been too much to have stolen a rose? Karel said.

I only walked through the maples and plucked one green leaf.

And in winter?

On my left I'd see frozen birds, frozen last night too, on my right the shadows of smoke on the sides of buildings. That's all.

Karel stood up and removed his coat. Do you realize he said that I am what you might call tight?

I'm sure it couldn't be that. Think of Camille Julian said. But he was a little tired too now. Was it his heart's large mouse that was eating away his insides? He thought bed would be a good place to go to. Since he had in his bag only one pair of pajamas he gave Karel the pants and took the coat for himself. They were black pajamas with white figures. While they undressed he thought Karel unimportantly dirty; before, he hadn't thought about hygiene and morals, both being easy to neglect.

Karel thought him just a little rustic.

The coat looked like a coat on Julian.

Karel's shoulders were spare but his chest was full and his arms round so he looked well in just the pants.

They decided that Karel sleep on the right side of the bed.

Julian lay on his back in the dark and inhaled cigarette smoke, accelerating his heart even more.

Karel breathed on his left side. The January moon must have been behind some tower. He said oh. I can't sleep now.

Why not there's nothing else to do Julian said.

Isn't there?

It's so late isnt it?

Well, your heart is beating very fast.

Much gin Julian murmured and turned on his left side also.

Are you really sleepy? Karel said.

Yes I am trying to decide what I shall dream about.

Or whom.

Yes. You can feel my left side thumping even extending the thump to my right side. I should much rather not be excited at all or excited much more. He placed the cigarette's lighted ash in the carpet, took a deep breath and embraced the pillow. Good night he said.

Karel was silent. Then before it is light I must do something cruel he said.

That I should say indicates a heat not submerged by the important Julian said.

Karel hesitated, then bloomed from the bed like a white four-o'clock. He snapped the light on and faced the mirror, looking into it closely and pressing his temples with long unshapely fingers. I am weak he said which is to say that on this planet there are many large people not being very kind and when one is not being killed being a little less than kind which is after all too social. I shall go out and I shall recite and I shall use high heels over their corpses and fail to vibrate with their throats' sweet words of me saying you are the darling of the Doll's House but I shall go further into that other house though still there and wait for what will come like the cracking of eggs on the sides of frying pans. He looked around and saw Julian lying on his stomach observing him with one wide eye.

He turned his back and shed the pajama pants and dressed not too slowly.

Julian lit a cigarette from the pack on the floor beside the bed-post. Karel will you be nice and repeat Frank's number he said.

It's in the directory Karel said.

You know the kind of eyes that have been drunk so often. Julian sat up in bed. Im sorry you won't stay.

To be inevitably misunderstood is a matter for armchair relaxation Karel said but to be unnecessarily misunderstood... he put his hand on the door-knob which felt cold as a forehead. The tunnel-like hall held his horizontal, the elevator going down his vertical moving. He went into the street, more darkened now, and went forward walking slower and slower until he stopped altogether in front of a bench in Washington Square and sat down with his mind prenatally blank.

...if you dream of it or if you don't dream of it there are loads of things to do. Yes said I working my way carefully past my mother's womb. How many are there? Before flowers or anything. How many are there? But flowers were and food and flowers were and. Let's do a bit of plain walking I said to my friend. We were not completely under the awning but we were almost under it. We were. I think that was myself. Very young maybe three. No.

Not three. Two. That might have been suffi-
cient. It might have been as it was that diphtheria
came and almost. But. How now that I think
after it all how can it come here now so really.
No question mark because I want to. It I
only know: it is a sweet party: it is. I am.
My suit is dainty and all of white and stockings
are being pulled on. Stockings are being pulled
on because or in spite of the first guest who is
in sight, walking with a nurse maid and I see
them for a moment as I am permitted a glimpse
(one stocking is still hanging). And so they
arrive. Solely. Twoly. Brilliantly fabu-
lous. I do not particularly care, once the ice
cream is over. I am five but I am allowed to
forget it. Until I want to count them and so I
stand them in a row: fifty-one guests and the
doll I got I got I got. I tear grass from the roots
on my fifth birthday lawn and they imitate me
the other children and I am glad. And they.
Are. Between this and that. I am afraid. Even
now. Between this and that there might have
been: or were: elephantine globularosities protect-
ing their own children like perfect mothers,
unaware that a child (I) of five (I) pranced, ran,
stumbled, uncared for except in. O elephantine
globularosities, who what are you if you are or
could be? Between this and that. I love hoops.
The round things of wood and sidewalks and
running and I am bought a hoop and I play with

it, running as I expected to run. But is it quite as I expected. I am afraid not. Nor was the Doll. I am not ashamed of my doll. Although it is kept because, I know, only little girls, high up in the big closet in its close glory. I never play with it. I want to show it to them once. But someone is it Grandmother is it Mother snatched SNATCHED it back to some sort of heaven I suppose but my heart. And a velocipede, and an English Mail. Yes, wheels. Hoops. The English Mail (there is an Irish Mail too) is kept in the hall and I want to take it out when it shouldn't be taken out and it is sometimes taken out on the hard asphalt the hard. *Knights rush over smooth grey ground. They fall.* There are races too. And other children. There is a picture of me when I was or am I how many years old then which pictures me as I am minus about the exact number of years. Life is bitter and head aches. I think there must be a place called Philadelphia for I am going there. There. School. Oh. I am going to school. The teachers put lumps of dark sugar into cups of hot water in the afternoons after school as I wait for my mother to take me home. It tastes salty like meat gravy I discover. Snow I ingest, snow I know, snow it is soft cold out of which one makes snowballs which the children throw at each other. There is a snowball battle but I do not like it. I do not make quite the right number of hits. And while in the cold during recess beside the snow over the ice children play it must be coldly I stick my nose above the window sill my mother having through teacher decreed I am to stay indoors. I AM TO STAY INDOORS. *Forever the great dark shall move with breasts offering but withholding stars planets alps one likes to climb or go through a valley skiing.* Or when children are out. I am impressed by the Horse Fair by Blankety Blank but I find something lacking in it. Is it the horses? Even bread and tea are good after a sickness. And a little cold lamb. I love my set of elaborate wooden Indians but I leave them in the sand for the rain to spoil for my tin soldiers who are smarter looking. I want the image of Kermit Roosevelt in a doll. I want it. I get it on Christmas morning. *Guinevere or Elaine is hanging from her window and stone is going downward beneath her and somehow her heart is fluttering terribly excited. What? Who? He. Lancelot or someone or who was it comes... comes... He has plumes... There are many noises in the air not of birds no of nothing but Lancelot.*

———

CHAPTER THREE: GABRIEL AND LOUIS

You must come and help me find a place to live Julian said leaning half out of bed to talk to Karel over the telephone at noon the next day when where was the sun.

Did you succeed Karel asked in forestalling realization?

That is not immediately thought of in fact whoever sells stamps in this hotel is sure to annoy me, won't you come by?

I'm not so used to benches on cement.

Don't you know any taxi-drivers?

If you insist on being impenetrable perhaps I could come by without risk of hurting your feelings.

Now when will it be I mean how long before—

Oh in an hour if I don't go back to bed I do feel pale blue as a friend of mine says of me which is mostly a mistake on his part.

Julian unwound the bedclothes from him and went to the window. Where *was* the sun? He thought it must be hiding its face in shame. He tried to see the sky and saw a part of it. The view consisted mostly of three walls of windows the majority with the shades up, all with the same kind of sad curtains either hanging straight or drawn back. A voice with a Western accent came from one of the lower windows *I've just gotten in but there are so MANY Fergusons in the phone book I thought maybe you could tell me*. She's probably brought the entire state of Texas with her and expects people not to know the difference Julian thought... He went to the washstand and shaved carefully, washed thoroughly, cleaned his teeth indifferently, combed his hair repeatedly, and put on his clothes. He looked at himself in the mirror from various angles and thought he would do.

Karel met him in the lobby. Did you steal fire from heaven last night?

To speak chronologically I'm afraid the vulture consumed my liver.

Tenth Street, Fifth Avenue, Washington Square were walked on.

We'll go to Simon's first Karel suggested.

Mr. Simon was in his office and breathed in puffs. Have you got *mon*ey? Can you pay your rent? Wait I'll show you a byootiful place. I'll fix it all up for you. Mr. Simon was noted for his minor philanthropies among the artists and the two women in his office, a mother and daughter who had never slept but together, tried to guard his interests and always showed their probably false teeth in a smile at most of the tenants. There was a young lady in one of his numerous houses once who had not paid her rent for eight months so Mr. Simon had her summoned to court. They were both there and the judge told the young lady she would have to move, whereupon she burst into tears. Mr. Simon was touched. He took her from the court room, hailed a taxi, brushed a tear from his own cheek, handed her a ten dollar bill and told her to stay in his house as long as she wanted to and not to mind what that old judge said.

Mr. Simon took Julian and Karel to Third Street under the elevated tracks. He stopped in front of what had been a batik shop but now the door was curtained and the cloudy windows draped halfway up. Inside was a large room with a balcony half across the width and extending the whole length. The balcony was reached by little stairs on the left and held a wide low bed and antique sofa. A partition from the balcony to the floor hid a kitchenette and a combination dressing-room and washroom; a further partition with two doors at right angles enclosed a comparatively brown toilet bowl and seat. In the room on the floor were a red leather couch (one arm missing), studio bed, built out fireplace, lamp, two chests of drawers, stool and two tables. The design on the grass carpet was indistinguishable.

Mr. Simon had been talking. I'll fix a shower-beth *he*re, put up nize *cur*tains, have the rug cleaned make it nize, put curtains across the bel-

cony rail, curtains here, it will be *vun*derful.
It was also going to be wonderful how long Julian
was to stay there without paying any rent after
the first month or so.

How much?

Fifteen dollars I've been getting but you can
have it for twelve.

A week?

Sure a vweek.

That's too much. The place will be occupied
by only myself.

Vwell, ten if you pay the ges and lights. I pay
the vwater.

Ten a week, do you think that's too much,
Karel?

Karel shrugged and pursed his lips. Someone
had told him don't purse your lips but he had said
where would I be if I had never pursed my lips?

I'll take it, Mr. Simon, when will it be fixed
up at least cleaned up?

This efternoon.

I'll be here tonight to sleep.

Very goodt. He gave him the key.

Thank you, Mr. Simon, won't you eat a hot
dog with 'is?

Noo thenks.

They ate hot dogs for breakfast. The wagon
was parked on the street in front of the door and
they bought bananas from a cart further down.

They went for Julian's trunk and brought it

back from the docks on the side of a taxi to 319 West Third Street.

There were no cooking utensils nor eating ones so they went to 'Tillie's' on Fourteenth Street which at five o'clock is a most vulgar street, invariably alive with the sex-starved.

First they had a pineapple delight served by a girl wearing a hairnet. Cups, saucers, knives, forks, spoons, plates, glasses, boilers, a skillet and a coffee pot were purchased at ten cents an article. Karel needed an eyebrow pencil which he bought at another counter from a salesgirl who looked mixed up.

Karel accompanied Julian to the hotel where the latter put on a dark blue overcoat, packed his bag and paid his bill, much to the relief of the personnel.

Fifth Avenue was dignified; Macdougal Street was marking spaces with taxis for a block that included tea-rooms and a dancing place where you got showerbaths one heard. Third Street divided Macdougal into this upper half and a lower half of gangsters, dark girls and children who played street games.

At 319 the lights were amber and when turned on could be seen from outside, giving the appearance of a speakeasy.

Julian's trunk delivered a typewriter, various books, a dressing gown, suits, and accessories, most of which were to be picked up.

Karel sat down and began typing a poem.

Julian said it's cold and drank two glasses of water. He felt the radiators and they were faintly warm. Come on let's go out and eat he said.

Karel continued to type.

Julian said I'm going.

Karel put his fallen hair in place and said all right wait.

Snow fell and left itself on their coats. They went to a coffee pot and ordered Western sandwiches and coffee. Karel spoke to two young men that came in. They walked up to the stools and spoke to Karel. He introduced them to Julian: Gabriel and Louis.

They were poets.

Gabriel was an Italian, born in New York. His hair wrapped around itself and had snowdrops in it for he was without a hat. He had black eyebrows that almost met in the center. His eyes were remote but his smile exhibited friendliness.

Louis wore a beret and his mouth was beginning to turn down at the corners. He was somewhat taller than Gabriel and sometimes held one shoulder lower than the other. Have you got a cigarette Karel? he asked. He had a deliberately soft voice.

The two remained standing.

Have one Julian said offering his package. Have something to eat.

They sat down on the stools.

It's too fucking cold to be running around trying to raise fifty dollars Gabriel said.

For what? Karel asked.

For an abortion Gabriel said.

Karel said how strange.

The four finished their sandwiches. Gabriel and Louis ate cheesecake also.

They went outside and stood on the corner of Eighth Street and Sixth Avenue. Louis spoke of the logic of Rimbaud; Gabriel of the rareness of faith, hence the preponderance of betrayals; Julian of a new poem he was contemplating in which time would be an evil to be forgotten; Karel of his uncomfortableness: I can't stand here shading my eyelashes all night.

Where are you living? Gabriel asked Julian.

Three nineteen West Third—the store place. Drop by some night.

The world holds few terrors anymore Louis said.

Are you going our way Karel? Gabriel asked.

No I'm not.

Karel and Julian left them standing on the corner. When they had crossed Fourth Street Karel said do not adopt them. I don't trust them. They are not to be tolerated. Remember, *do* not. They are magnificent in the abstract but in the concrete dangerous.

You say they have acted.

They are always acting and are not always scientific.

They reached Julian's place and went in.

Karel's tie which he wore in a wide loop knot low on a collar that stopped at his throat's end always became disarranged when he removed his overcoat. That partly accounted for his endurance record in front of the mirror. Sentimentality he said is a willingness to believe in form without substance.

Then Gertrude Stein—

Stein ha I think she ought to float away in space and start her own universe.

What about Gabriel and Louis?

Oh Gabriel revolted at twenty-one from the teachings of a Franciscan monastery and Louis is the son of a Rabbi so they are now complete anarchists.

Whom else do you know?

Mostly people who splash around like children in bathtubs.

No one would expect the ocean to be subdued under such circumstances. Have you seen Theodosia lately?

To be inexact I saw her with Windward and his crowd the other night at Noe's. I swooned in and began my first poem saying *crape*, heavily, as I looked directly at her, but it is not less than profane that we agree on some things and she had a sweet face.

Is she living with Windward?

No. You knew her in San Francisco?

Yes I knew her. She knows that I have planned to be here and I must call her tomorrow.

Is it really that imminent?

Suppose you ask Windward and the rest around and I'll ask Theodosia and we'll have a party.

You'd better have curtains put up first for policemen and such might burst in with suspicions.

I'll see Simon.

All right, I suppose I'll drag my body homeward angel.

Must you?

I have an unusual appointment for tomorrow afternoon and there may be developments so to speak.

Until tomorrow then.

When Karel had gone Julian, resting his chin in one hand, felt the blood rock his head. He went to his couch and thought of someone else who wasn't himself but a little boy whose grandmother ate dinner with him. He went home with her and on the way they met a negro boy with a billy-goat. The goat was on the sidewalk and it butted his grandma.

I got sent out of the room by Brother Austin for he thought I hit a boy with a piece of chalk but I didn't. Today is my birthday. Mammy baked me a big birthday cake. I wrote a poem called *What's the Use?* Sister and I went downtown to Kress's. We were looking at some valentines when a negro girl who was trying to steal a dime bank was caught by a lady detective. I sailed my kite in Jones' field after school. It got tangled up with another boy's and fell just as I had let out all my string. Sister has two little chickens; they are painted orange and pink but the pink one looks sick. Mother and I went down to the river to see how high the water is; it covers the roofs of some of the houses on mud island. Sister's pink chicken died. Martin and I got in a fight after school. Brother Leopold said we must sit on the monkey-box every noon for a month. The nightingales and mocking-birds played ball; the mocking-birds won 18 to 13. I'm a mocking-bird but lost my base-ball. Himogle-boogley. I had to stay in after school for laughing. When the queen tried to christen the viaduct by passing over it in an aeroplane and dropping a bottle of champagne on it she missed by several feet. I went out to Mr. Bass's to have my wart conjured off. I am going away to school. I love my mother so much I am thinking of her all the time.

I am getting long pants and things and kissing people I don't want to for instance Theodosia whom I love for poetry's sake but how did I know I was beautiful enough to make her hold her breasts tightly and afterwards say with her mind do you know where bottomless places are and their reality? did you ever have to go down to the blank wall of death (I have died so often life seems stiff and awkward she said) and when you were there find even reality a little forced? Because of hunger she said which is like feeling blood flow until the last drop is chilled with wind upon the pavement.

Theodosia with her disquieting beauty, sarcasm, violated eyes. Theodosia walking in sunlight, walking in morning, walking in sun paths, walking, walking and walking and saying of age: I am not old enough, I am too young. Theodosia walking in sunlight, walking on dead grass, bearing her body through the sunlight over the dead grass. Theo. Theodosia drinking the morning, drinking the noon, Theo in moonlight, in darkness, walking, walking and saying he is queer. I wonder. Theo bearing wonder. Theodosia finding queer, saying I love you. In strange smoke-thick yellowed air of speakeasies, over wine, over liqueurs, over smoke, over dreamings, Theodosia chanting words like broken musics: I love you. In the yellow afternoon of blinding heat Theodosia in orchid, white limbs and amber hair, white limbs and scarlet shoes, white limbs as nude as morning, Theo in orchid. Theo finding *queer*: walking slowly in sunlight and saying slowly: I almost believe, except there is a difference and if you are? then there IS a difference. Theodosia walking in sunlight of morning bearing her pale not virgin body over spent dreamings, bearing her pale not virgin body and slim limbs, walking and walking in sunlight and saying queer, I love you. Theodosia walking in sunlight, walking in morning while there is yellow over houses, yellow over half-dreams, yellow over amber hair, and yellow through which Theodosia is walking. Theodosia will say I love you. She will say more surely: I love you through the blue smoke and yellow air of speakeasies. Theo will be walking, walking, walking, bearing her pale slim not virgin body her white slender limbs through my after-dreams somehow always.

———

CHAPTER FOUR: THE FIGHT

WHEN Julian awoke afternoons he could look up through the top of the front windows as he lay on his back and see the people in the elevated cars go by. Later he could see them too: the lighted windows moving successively like a strip of film. He didn't know how many seconds the eyes of the people in the cars could focus on him at night eating with a candle on the table or reading or writing a poem when he was not very happy.

This evening he was expecting Karel at eight. At ten minutes after nine the glass was tapped twice and he went to the door, pulled aside the curtains to look out haughtily, then pulled back the bolt.

Karel said he had been detained at the communist cafeteria in Union Square. A bantamweight prizefighter whom he used to know last year had renewed his acquaintance. He wants me to introduce him to some girls so I told him to come by tomorrow night for the party. He's the type that will bring along a friend too.

Julian poured out glasses of red Italian wine bought down the street before dinner.

Karel walked about the room smoking, as his

habit was, without inhaling. Julian saw a bracelet on his left wrist. Let me look at your bracelet.

Karel took it off and handed it to him. My jewel boxes will be bursting if last night should be repeated often.

What happened?

When I went uptown I found Vincent and Tony with a crowd there. Of course I went directly to the bathroom and retouched my face and if I do say so I was—not that life hadn't had a big new howlong? thrill—

Yes my dear but in our anarchistic universe can we have everything we want even for one little minute: I mean for a special dreadful reason, but as far as one's own orgasm goes have you concluded that that is the *less* important?

Not at all times because bracelets can become symbols. There was an old thing there in evening clothes who whispered something in my ear and since I couldn't pretend to be awfully shocked we went upstairs... To my amazement I was told to go back and send Vincent up and to my utter exhaustion when Vincent came down there was a second request for me...

And just for cold lucre?

Oh it's not so cold after all no not so—but listen to this: after that happened Gabriel and Louis came by not having any place to sleep. They were contemptuous as usual and began insulting everyone but Vincent and Tony and me in an unmistakable manner so the others took their sables and flew.

Something is always threatening trade...

Yes or trade... We decided to have some food before going to bed, I was to sleep there, and Louis was selected to fetch it from the delicatessen. Tony, the impulsive Latin, offered Louis his new camel's-hair coat because of the cold, Louis had only a muffler. Louis admired the coat out loud, put it on and hasn't returned until yet. Tony poor thing is looking for him with a knife. I suppose I should have warned Tony but it all happened so quickly and besides once he has his mind on something...

There was a loud knock on the glass and Julian parted the curtains. It's them.

Who?

Gabriel and Louis.

He opened the door and they came in.

Where is your coat? Karel asked looking at Louis.

Have a cigarette Louis said offering a small box of Benson & Hedges. He had a fresh haircut.

Oh said Karel prosperity...

Gabriel made himself at home by selecting a book from the row on the table. It was an anthology of modern poetry. These dopes Pound and Eliot... he began.

Listen Louis said reclining on the window-seat talk about something primary such as how we're going to raise some cash before you find yourself a father.

Julian said are you still trying to raise that money? How are you eating in the meantime?

Christ there are too many ways Louis said. The easiest is by asking people on the street.

I suppose their reactions *wouldn't* be identical Karel said.

Take that fuck McAllen. What do you suppose he thought when I followed him to a gin-mill, walked up to him before he could take his first drink and said McAllen I think your poetry is lousy but I need a buck.

Did you get it?

Hell, yes, he gave me two and I gave him back half of it and said I asked for only one.

You are a panic Julian said. When I get completely broke I'll try that.

But the beautiful thing is the response of some of the cunts Louis continued. The young ones are insulted to think that a man would want to take money from them. The old ones usually come across with at least a quarter.

Don't any of them ever call a cop?

Why should they? I borrowed a dollar from a cop I had never seen before last night. A cop wouldn't do anything about that. Although once I had the unfortunate inspiration to tell a woman what an ugly dog she had after she refused to give me money. She called a dick and I was taken to Bellevue for examination. I ended up by examining the doctors and getting a loan from them.

My dear you are simply insurmountable Karel said.

Louis had the habit, borrowed from Gabriel, of exhaling cigarette smoke with a vicious sound —of impatience no doubt. Say Julian how about my taking a bath here he said.

If you want to. The shower is upstairs.

I know. Simon is asleep at this hour. Have you a towel?

Yes, there's one in the washroom there.

Are you writing anything now Gabriel? Karel said.

Gabriel kept his overcoat on. I'm working on a play Karel he said.

What is it?

Not exactly worked out yet but about a man who is arrested for kissing a little girl on the street. He had an impulse to kiss her for no reason either of tenderness or fetichism.

Louis had stripped to the waist and was about to ask for some soap when there was another knock on the door.

Julian looked out at a face he didn't recognize.

Karel looked out too and said it's Edwin.

Jesus Christ Louis said.

Julian let the curtain fall back and said let him in?

Hell Louis said.

Don't let him in said Gabriel.

What's the matter? Karel asked.

Louis said shit let him in.

Julian opened the door.

Edwin stepped in. Is Louis here? he asked. He was dressed in what could be called only a costume. His overcoat was open showing buff-colored pants, a velvet jacket, open collar and black windsor tie. He also had a jaw. His flat face was set to express anger but his lips were too pouty for him to appear more than poetic.

Yes I'm here Edwin. Do you want to see me? Louis crossed his arms.

I've come to get that dollar you took from Geraldine or take it out of your hide.

Yeah? Louis smiled with half his mouth.

I mean it damn it. He seemed on the point of tears as he removed his overcoat and looked at Louis. He turned to Karel and Julian who appeared unsympathetic and said I've tried to avoid this but Louis has deceived and stolen from my Love. He promised to pay back the dollar and he hasn't done it. I'm going to teach him a lesson like I said I would or try anyway.

All right Louis said I haven't a dollar. Do you want a fight?

Yes! Edwin took off his jacket, removed his tie and shirt and laid them in a neat pile on the table.

Louis began warming up by punching at the air as soon as he saw Edwin's muscular back and good arms. Edwin was also the taller.

Are you ready? Edwin asked, blushing.

Keep time for them Julian Gabriel said. Fight one-minute rounds, I'll referee.

This is terrible! Karel said shaking his bracelet above his head.

Go! cried Julian, hoping that Louis would win.

They went: Louis feinting and attacking, Edwin standing and punching Louis' head. At the end of the first minute Louis threw himself on the floor, breathing hard. Edwin sat on the bed going over the details as to just why he had to do this and also telling Louis that he was dissipated and hadn't been leading the right kind of life. He said I used to box in the navy you know. Do you want another round or have you had enough?

Louis was furious and got to his feet. You bastard! he said. He was more on the defensive now but every time he struck at Edwin the latter hit him in the face. Louis attacked him wildly with blows from both fists, and found himself lying across the couch after sinking into blackness and blinding light and rising again.

Karel rushed to the washroom for a towel and cold water.

Edwin was apparently more satisfied than he intended to be.

Gabriel fanned Louis and rubbed his hands.

Edwin said I'd give him a dollar myself if I had it but I have to work for my living.

In those clothes? Gabriel asked.

I write poetry too. But I have a sense of decency. I hope I haven't hurt him. But he insulted my Love, you see...

I'm afraid I don't see said Gabriel.

I see said Julian but I'm sure I *don't* know your face.

Edwin put his clothes back on and took his departure. The others were silent.

Karel bathed Louis' face.

I'm all right Louis said. Give me a cigarette. I didn't know the son-of-a-bitch could fight.

Anything else he might do would be superfluous Karel said.

Louis got up with a few swollen places on one cheek and on his forehead and lips. I guess I'll take the bath now.

A guy like that with dementia praecox ought to be secretly disposed of Gabriel said.

His earnestness was amazing said Julian.

He's a beast Karel said.

Julian gave Louis soap and handed him the towel.

I'll be back soon Louis said, his back looking a little rounder than it had.

Still writing poetry? Gabriel asked Karel when Louis had gone.

What is one to do but face the inevitable?

I'm going to do some sociological and ethnological work.

Do you mind if I ask you a *Little Review* question?

No—I don't.

Do you write because it pleases you?

Yes, I do. But you should read my essay on art. Gabriel half closed his eyes.

Yes? I suppose you put art in its place?

Well, you might call it that.

That's all right... I don't mind granting anyone his prerogative to think that way—but then I insist on reminding him that there *is* such a thing as sociology said Karel.

I have decided that poetry is prose with an inferiority complex Gabriel said.

Yes but—Julian put in.

Man prattles poetry and writes prose... Prose I think is the truly aristocratic art.

But the adult is a convention which may be ignored—or valuably misunderstood. Poetry, like prose, is concerned with aesthetic. It's a question of value, purely. Julian felt prouder after saying this.

Gabriel is merely being abnormally oblique Julian Karel said. How would it feel he said to Gabriel for you to consider meaning instead of being meant?

I went through all that last week. You've

heard the expression to have the shit scared out
of you. Such a thing was demonstrated to me
to be based on truth... About dawn I was
walking along Fourth Street when a car of four
gangsters who had come out of the coffee pot on
Fourth and Sixth drove toward me. They saw
me and called out hey faggot! as they passed
by. I kept walking but when I heard them turn
the car around I started to run. They sped up
and were even with me when I ran inside a building I knew and locked myself in the toilet in the
back of the hall. I was just in time for both
the locking of the door and the toilet... I
suppose I would have been raped by those
bastards.

Karel opened his mouth into an oval and his
eyes became wide. My God Gabriel think of
me! Oh, the fiends! He lay down on the couch.

Julian said are they that dangerous?

They were probably drunk or I don't see how
they mistook *me*...

Yes you do have a face like a truck-driver.

Louis came in the side door from upstairs naked.

My God did you come through the hall that
way? Julian exclaimed.

Yes... little good it did.

Exhibitionist! Julian said.

Karel slid from the couch. How do your
bruises feel? he said to Louis touching his cheek
with a finger.

All right. They're all right. Are there any more cigarettes?

There's some listerine in the cabinet would that help them Julian said or vaseline?

Do you want some vaseline on them Louis? Karel asked.

No they'll be all right. I'm tired. He stretched out on the bed and closed his eyes. His body was smooth and lightly olive like his face.

Karel Julian thought was over-solicitous.

After a few minutes Louis got up and began to dress.

Gabriel rose, put out his cigarette and sat down on the couch by Julian.

Karel and Louis were in the washroom.

Gabriel looked at Julian and said I'd like to walk with you through terrible things happening.

Julian regarded his mouth and insincere eyes. My bed will never be wide enough he said.

Louis came out of the washroom and said to Gabriel let's get out of here.

Karel came out with his hat on. Julian looked at him.

I'll see you tomorrow night Karel said. Did you call Theodosia?

Yes.

The three left together and Julian lay on his back waiting to look up. He thought about the dawn and wondered if it would come too soon. There he was wondering as he would

3

wonder yes as he would wonder at eighty if he should live that long or must he wonder to live making the if bad form. He believed in the bird swaying on the bough.

But where was paradise? What if he had something in his eye. Oh to be Prometheus sex-guy and whore-walloper what if he had something in his eye there *was* something in. He went to the mirror and held his eye opened until it watered. Did he ever *know* anyone to hark back back hark and one lies up some stairs who did surprisingly. He put his coat on and his hat on and locked the door behind him.

The fine snow was fine and there was a man he saw hugging an ash can. He crossed Seventh Avenue and turned into Commerce Street. He found the number and looked up at a dark window. He went in the house and up the stairs without making any noise. His feet made blank sounds on the linoleum in the hall.

Gabriel and Louis had gotten a room in the same building with Karel. Karel's room was next door to theirs. He told them he was sleepy and left them.

In his own room after a while he thought he knew. He thought he knew he didn't quite know. But he knew. He would imagine he knew; that was just as good.

Instead of undressing and getting into bed he walked into the hall and knocked on their door.

That was quite possible for him to do he thought; it was possible because they knew it was just possible. So there he was; in it; in the room.

Louis and Gabriel were stretched half-clothed on top of the bed. Some garments, very dirty, were flung about with a recklessness which Karel marked, the recklessness that was truly artistic.

Karel was on his guard with them; he felt a bit self-conscious because he had not been kind to them. Louis' trousers, drawn up by short suspenders, attracted him as his skin had attracted him at Julian's. Louis' face above a black sweater with a white mooncurved wide stripe draped over the chest was alive. Now, as mostly, as always almost, Louis conveyed thoughtfulness to him, thoughtfulness now behind a bruised mouth, and behind eyes. He permitted himself to look at Louis as he had thought of seeing him when on the other side of the wall. Yes he thought.

Louis' activity was in his favor. In repose his face was dark, even morbid. When smiling it attracted because it was evil and young. Moreover, Karel saw that his smile gave his jaw the correct proportion, the without which not beauty, in spite of the swollen spot on his cheek. He sat down by Louis' outstretched form and was gratified to have him move closer to him.

Gabriel and Louis were waiting. They were waiting for their good fortune to occur, to come with the dawn; they were going to force the world to be good with them. They did not want it to be good to them for it could not be good to them who were too good for anyone to be good to them but the world was stupid enough to be punished. It was stupid enough to be fooled; and they had to live.

Karel knew that he was not the world, for he had come into their room then; the world had not done that; the world only put its hands into its pockets when asked, Gabriel and Louis had asked Karel; he had refused. But he was changing, he was changing from the world into something else And they had known that he could change. But would he? Well, they would know very shortly, and on whose account he was changing.

Karel's hand strayed over the rough sweater's surface and landed on Louis' warm neck. His heart gave a leap. Yes! it said. Karel was doing this because he knew it could be done.

Louis looked at Gabriel and caught at Karel's hand, putting it onto his chest under the sweater.

Karel's tight heart grew less tight. It must be what time and he had not slept. Now he could afford to remain awake a little longer. With Gabriel and Louis. But only Louis should profit. As he must profit. As Karel was willing he should profit, anyway at first, for that was the only way it could be done. Just a little Karel thought Gabriel sensed that. But they must both be jubilating, they must both be thinking this.

He kissed Louis. Louis urged him.

Karel was enjoying the progress. It must be so now. It could be his way. So he was not completely responsive. He sat up. I want a cigarette if you have one.

Sure said Louis and produced one from a creased package.

What about something to eat? Gabriel asked.

Let the food go. I'm not hungry Louis said.

Gabriel glanced heavily at him, then disgust spread over his face, a light disgust. I want coffee he said but indifferently.

Karel said I have no money.

Louis lay smoking.

Then I'm going to sleep. I don't care what you guys do Gabriel said. He turned over, away from them.

Past the window there was gray-filled space soon to be practically blue. Karel walked to the window and looked out. He turned around to look at Louis and then walked quietly over and sitting by his head on the bed asked him, in a whisper, if he wished to sleep in his room.

Sure Louis said. He beheld Gabriel's back. His mouth curled. His eyes assumed vacancy as he flung his cigarette mightily away beyond the window.

In Karel's room Karel's heart beat faster. This was this, taking Louis into his room, separating him from Gabriel. Louis would not care about him any longer. No; he could afford to do nothing for Gabriel Karel thought.

The sheets were absolutely cold. Louis was waiting in them.

Their arms were around each other, the light was on, they stared at the ceiling. Later Louis slept, the light was off, a fear was on his heart, Karel's heart, he was awake. Then the door was knocked on and he heard Karel Karel.

What? Who is it?

It's Julian. Let me in.

The door opened and Karel's astonished face said what's the matter? Come in what's the matter? Darling!

Julian went in the tiny room and Karel turned the light on. Louis was apparently still asleep.

I have something in my eye. I couldn't sleep. I must go to a doctor. Will you take me to one?

But Julian I don't know of any doctor's office open at this hour Karel said let me see your eye.

Julian went to the lamp and opened his eye can you see anything?

No but it looks blood-shot.

Come on out with me and we'll have breakfast. I'll see a doctor later on.

I'll have to dress. He was in his underwear.

He looked at Louis without any explanation to Julian.

Julian looked at his eye again in the mirror and said God.

Karel said what could be in it?

Something must.

Oh how terrible Karel said.

Julian said a hot punchino would be good. Karel said it would too so they went to Frankie's. They ordered punchinos from the partly cross-eyed waiter with a German accent.

There was a group of men and a round blonde girl at the next table. One of the men went over and said to Karel isn't your name Karel and aren't you a writer and won't you both join our table?

Karel and Julian would.

They had applejack. Eventually one pulled out a poem and asked Karel to criticize it. Karel did, doing justice he thought to everything.

Shortly after putting back his poem, another drink having been consumed, the same one pulled out his wallet and showed Karel a card attached therein which read Soandso HONORARY CHIEF OF POLICE.

Karel said were you really in the police department?

The man pulled aside his coat and showed him a badge on his belt. Come over to see me in New Jersey any time he said. Then he thought another drink would be distinctly in order and left to get a bottle from the bar. Whereupon, the blonde round girl having got up to dance with the second man at the table, the third man at the table leaned over to Julian and said I would like to rape that girl there before everybody's eyes.

Julian got over that neatly because when the girl came back she sat on his lap.

The men decided they would go so they all went outside including Karel and Julian and the girl who said let's continue the party at my place.

They all went with her and not having a thing to do decided to play strip poker. They counted their things and every deal the low man removed an article.

The girl, after a while, was almost undressed at the same time that Julian was almost fully clothed. They were playing on a sheet on the floor. She made them promise not to make her remove her shorts but when her brassières came off they knew there was no wind to make the shorts stay on.

Julian at last began to see that it wouldn't be long for him either. When he was nude the girl said I'm drunk and laid her head in his lap.

Finally everyone left the girl's apartment except Karel and Julian and the three slept in one bed, Julian having forgotten about breakfast and all about his eye.

CHAPTER FIVE: THE PARTY

THE next night Julian was expecting people he knew and people he did not know. He had told those he knew to come by for a raid-party and they were prepared to be taken to the station in the Black Maria. He had borrowed a portable victrola from Theodosia. She had records of Duke Ellington's timed primitiveness, King Oliver's trumpets and clarinets and Bennie Moten's natural rhythms.

Julian wore a black shirt and light powder-green tie. His dark hair had been washed to a gold brown and fell over his forehead.

Karel, as he had promised, came by three hours before the others bringing his box of beauty that included eyelash curlers, mascara, various shades of powder, lip and eyebrow pencils, blue and brown eyeshadow and tweezers for the eyebrows.

Julian submitted to his artistry, only drawing the line at his eyebrows being plucked.

I'll make you up to the high gods Karel said to the *high*... When he was through he regarded the result with a critical and gratified eye. Julian's rather full mouth now had lips which though less spiritual were not quite lewd. His eyes were simple sins to be examined more closely or to be looked at only from a distance.

Karel never did badly by his own face. He put an infinitesimal spot of lip salve in each nostril and almost invisible lines of black running vertically in the center of each eyelid. His eyelashes, as Frederick Spitzberger always predicted, were long enough now to catch in the boughs (should he go for a walk in Washington Square). His mouth, though not long, was made smaller sometimes by his raising the lower lip and pushing in the upper lip with it. Of course his eyebrows often looked the same as the week before. They could be pencilled into almost any expression: Clara Bow, Joan Crawford, Norma Shearer, etc. He thought he would choose something obvious for tonight. Purity.

Julian said you stay here while I go for the gin.

Don't be gone forever Karel said applying a liquid to his hair which would make a deep wave when properly set.

Why *do* you hold your lips that way? Julian called from the door.

Because I think it looks adorable Karel answered.

Julian went out into the freezing air. He would buy the gin at the Dragon Tavern. He walked fast, though remaining wholly conscious of the green yellow and black taxis cruising with the promise of anything.

It was Saturday night and the Tavern was

crowded. Vivian the blonde girl of the night before was there: starry-eyed: with grappa she said after she had disentangled herself from her dancing partner and gone over to Julian insisting that she pay back the fifty cents she had borrowed earlier that day for Kotex. Julian took it and said he might be back later. Rose, the Jewess who owned the place, handed him a package containing two bottles. He paid her and left.

At the studio he found that Frederick Spitzberger had arrived. Frederick was talking in a deep voice that was more often than not jarring; and always shocking when one considered Frederick's body: emaciated, with practically no shoulders and less hips and waist. As for his face, the nose was born he said and the body grew on later. His lips were prominent and curved outward. The shell-rimmed glasses he wore partly concealed his eyebrows: pencilled lines. And would who know that he used mascara around his small brown tender eyes that belied the caustic (though witty as he often said himself) dicta that he let fall upon the heads of others. His accent, which was quite correct, prevailed in whatever situation. He was smoking a black cigarette with a gold tip when Julian came in. In the washroom he was saying to Karel... his sneaky imperatives the slut forgets that the thing on which his assurance and hopes are built, commercial value, has much more substantiation in responsible sources in *my* case than in *his*: he refuses to recognize that I have contributed paid articles to four organs of literary expression rated officially as *A* among literary periodicals, all these beyond his reach; and that for about six hours' expert appraisal of manuscripts for purely commercial publishers I have made as much as a hundred and twelve dollars and fifty cents. Any illiterate who tries to denounce me for trying to be different because I can't be effective in any other way will get something like that information on his behind. Where do these self-appointed poetasting arbiters of middle-west poetic destiny think they come off?

When Julian slammed the door Frederick came out with an eyebrow raised and said this must be little boy blue.

Julian said how do you do?

Karel came from the washroom looking resplendent. I told K-Y to bring some goods to tack over the rest of the front windows. I'm desperately afraid of a raid.

Let's have a drink now Julian said unwrapping the High & Dry.

Yes indeed said Frederick starting *A Good Man is Hard to Find* on the phonograph.

While Julian was pouring the drinks Armand Windward came in with K-Y who was holding a bundle of red curtains under her arm. K-Y was from Kentucky. She lived with Windward in a sky-lit apartment and they took sunbaths in the nude regardless of visitors or the weather. Usually the only visitor was Frederick. K-Y was mistress of much flesh: breasts and hips in perfect lavish proportion. Her face was striking without makeup though occasionally she made more decided with a black pencil the point of hair growing at the top of her forehead. She was expansive and somewhat worthy of love. Artists drew her body. She did portraits of children. As for Windward, he always reserved the right to be whimsical; in fact, demanded the privilege when he had just the right amount of marijuana, the 'portorican papers' he bought on 99th Street.

Here are the curtains K-Y said I didn't bring any more on account of I didn't have any more.

Julian put the smaller table up on the window-seat and Karel climbed up on it and K-Y handed him thumb-tacks one at the time. People passing by outside slowed down, especially if they belonged to the unemployed, and looked up at him stretching the red curtains across the windows. He saw Santiago, a Mexican dancer whom he had asked to come, crossing the street with Osbert Allen, an English painter of American sky-scrapers. Sometimes at the Dragon Tavern Santiago danced the native dances he had learned in Mexico, to see them the following season introduced in a Broadway show 'for the first time in America'. Karel thought about him last summer at the artists' colony in Woodstock: a crowd had a bonfire by the pool one night making steak sandwiches and drinking applejack. Mrs. Dodge, wife of the philosopher, was there and Santiago with a rather extraordinary girl morbidly in love with him; also Karel and Osbert among others. For some trivial slight on Santiago's part the girl stalked away from the fire and down off into the darkness and to the icy pool where she pulled off her clothes and plunged in. It seems she had enacted such a performance before and the last time she was dragged out in a fainting frozen condition. So Osbert this time went after her. Santiago was very careless and only after much jockeying was persuaded to go down and help him get her out. When she wouldn't obey Santiago's command to come out he stripped and went in and began to yelp because of the cold—while she was blandly floating around, one supposed until she would be too exhausted to remain on top. As Santiago went toward her (Osbert had a flashlight playing on the pool) she fainted in his arms and he yelled for help because they were both sinking and freezing. They were near a rock in the middle of the stream and Osbert leaped out to it and dragged her on it and started massaging her. Then after exhortations from the shore she was passed with much difficulty from rock to rock and taken in a blanket back to the fire—weeping

and protesting that she wanted to swim and swim.
A scene followed between her and Santiago. She
bit his leg and he slapped her on the face. Almost
everybody chimed in on the argument. Mrs.
Dodge called Santiago, 'stinking shit'. Strange as
it may seem, Karel came out with admiration
for Santiago, regret over the girl, and disgust for
nearly everybody else. And he did a poem on it.

Osbert and Santiago entered during the cries
of Karel who had turned to lay Frederick out for
smoking a cigarette of marijuana. Frederick
said that he was his own mother and please,
Karel, after all.

The curtains were up and when Gabriel and
Louis came in, though they had not been invited,
Julian went to fix some more drinks. He came
out to hear Frederick ask of Louis where are
you bleeding? You must be bleeding somewhere for the groans you are emitting.

Osbert was already well filled with wine which
he drank habitually in large quantities. Santiago,
after dancing at the Tavern, had been known to
find Osbert on the floor of a wine cellar in need
of Physical Aid (though not Financial since
Osbert was to take Santiago on a European tour
the next summer). Osbert interrupted the
cockney story he was telling K-Y to giggle
profusely at Frederick's rebuke to Louis.

Julian asked who wanted gin and who didn't
want gingerale.

Another knock came and the door was opened to admit Karel's sandy-haired bantam-weight. The friend he introduced was also a boxer but was studying at New York University. He was in the light-weight class. The small one's name was Gene and he immediately offered K-Y a drink of rye which he carried in his hip-pocket. She said she wasn't drinking.

At last Theodosia came. Julian kissed her saying darling. Her once long hair had been shortened to a bob shaped to her head. She looked younger he thought or at least as young as she had looked two years before, although the circles under her eyes seemed to be permanent.

Yes she wanted a drink. She had been trying she said to make a decision all day and she would get drunk and make it.

Santiago in his consciously childish way said that he wanted something to eat and that he was bored. I'm bored he said and Theodosia was charmed with him.

Karel had forgotten about the dreaded raid and was talking to Louis on the apparent incongruity of having a very elaborate structure fall into oblivion at the (logically possible?) pulling of a trigger or cessation of heart-beat.

Julian put on a screaming record to drown out Frederick who had just said to Gabriel after a philosophical speculation on the latter's part: get off that pot, Annie, it's full of shit already.

Armand was well on his third marijuana and felt warmly decayed. Frederick asked him to dance.

Gene attached K-Y and was serious dancing with her large body in his arms.

Theodosia was with Gene's friend.

Julian led Karel in a slow dance step and Karel leaned—oh way back, and when the music stopped Gene's friend asked Karel if he could have the next one.

Julian and Theodosia went behind the partition for another drink. Theodosia liked to get drunk all at once so she took a double one. When they came out they found Gene trying to carry K-Y up the balcony steps but she was too heavy and the steps too narrow and since she wouldn't walk up and said Christ you're hurting me he had to be content with talking to her on the couch.

Somebody knocked. Karel went to the window and said it's Harold.

Harold Forte who illustrated books and bathrooms made his vivacious entrance and kissed almost everybody except Gabriel and Louis. He had on spats and a new suit since he had just returned from Philadelphia, having made he said oh hundreds and hundreds of dollars and having lived in the lap of luxury in a home which he 'did' for two weeks. Aren't the Villagers amusing? he remarked to Karel looking over his shoulder at Louis and Gabriel. Theo, dear, you look marvelous how do you do it ? Oh I must have some eggsie-weggsies I'm plastered. Julian dear how are you the last time I saw you you had one circle under each eye and now you have two.

That's a lie said Julian.

Frederick was appalled by what he termed Harold's vulgarity and said what can one do about people who are always trying to legitimatize their faces.

Frederick dear, *dear* Frederick... and nobody has introduced me to those ones Harold said indicating Gene and his friend.

Karel introduced them.

So charmed Harold said and then in a loud whisper to Santiago: Really who *are* these people— have they no homes ? At that Santiago had one of his painful laughing spells.

I say said Osbert to Harold you look positively gay in the new clothes.

Oh said Harold you're lovely *too*, dear, and gave him a big kiss on the forehead, much to Osbert's dismay. Then everybody became alarmed over Santiago who couldn't stop laughing between gasps for breath.

Julian thought that after all Gabriel and Louis were guests since they were there and asked Louis who was looking with his chin down at him if he wouldn't have a drink. Louis said he would and they retired. Things never happen to me Julian Louis said. I must always make things happen to other people. I'd like someone to take me by the hair... But Julian didn't and when they came out Julian saw Theodosia looking more surprised than hurt as Frederick said to her listen, disastrous, starting with a poem the conclusion is response, but starting with a poem is starting with a *poem* and the response is not the same as the response to an elephant.

Harold was getting Santiago off again with so I said to the Duchess—Dutch you old battleaxe *you* hold the baby for a while, my hands are wet.

Karel saw Julian and Louis together and thought he's the last stand surely my last stand if one won't be the whole exclusive flesh won't be the marble like that...

Gabriel took Louis aside and said let's go but Louis said not now.

The gin was all gone and Harold volunteered to buy two more bottles (even if he had sent all his money to his mother) provided someone else would go for it so Frederick said he would go for it with Gene's friend and Gene's friend not being articulate enough to say he'd rather not, went out the door with Frederick.

Armand's eyes were beginning to be red and dilated and glazed and K-Y called him honey over and over.

Julian and Theodosia danced and Theodosia spoke of things which might please her.

Harold was talking to Santiago and Osbert.

Karel was listening to Gabriel and Louis who were arguing about one thing while they meant another.

Frederick and Gene's friend came back sooner than everyone had expected and gin was drunk by everyone except K-Y and Gabriel.

Karel drank more than he had ever drunk in one evening.

The others were talking at the tops of their voices when there was a knock on the door leading into the hall and upstairs.

Oh God who could that be Karel said you go to the door Julian.

Julian opened the door as Karel and Frederick fled to the washroom.

Standing outside was a kimona with a head of hair sticking out the top. 'Please' came from a mouth that Julian did not locate at once. He gradually made out the eyes. If you're going to keep up this noise till morning *I'm* going to call the police. Ive got to go to work in Brooklyn at four o'clock and I've got to get some sleep whatdoyouthinkthisistheFOURTHOFJULY?

It does make me think of history Julian said have a drink.

No I won't have a drink and if you don't stop this noise I'm going to call the police call the police that's all me gottogotoworkat four o'clock way out to Brooklyn and you trying to tear the house down... She receded toward the stairs still talking and so up the stairs, still talking...

The nerve Harold said instead of apologizing for her face she asks us can you the nerve of...

Julian thought it best to at least stop the victrola since no one seemed inclined to leave just at that moment.

Everybody had another drink and when Karel passed out Julian allowed Frederick to put him to bed there. Frederick worshipped Karel and considered him his 'first influence'.

Gabriel urged Louis to leave with him. Louis said say wait a minute can't you? and Gabriel departed.

Theodosia said to Julian she had planned to spend the night with him but since Karel...

Yes Julian said since Karel...

Gene offered to take her home and Theodosia said all right call a taxi.

Can we sleep in the bed on the balcony? Osbert asked meaning Santiago and himself. I'm so drunk he won't be able to take me home.

Shut up Santiago said. I'll get you home you bore me.

Harold said he would die if he didn't have some oysters at once. So kissing (almost everybody) good-bye declaring, though, that his love was not wholly physical he left with Osbert and Santiago.

K-Y was still calling Armand honey and after a while got him to get up and go.

Frederick said his mother would be frantic if

he wasn't in soon but that he would see them tomorrow night. He lived in the Bronx.

Karel looked as if he would be unconscious until daylight.

Louis, the only other one left, had made no move to go so Julian said let's finish the gin. He drank his highball slowly and noticed for the first time what a beautiful nose Louis had. But he thought Louis' hair too thick as he grasped a handful. Julian looked at Louis looking up at him and said the only thing I have against life is that it spoils young men's mouths. Where are you sleeping tonight?

I have a place to sleep.

Sleep here. You and Karel and I will sleep in one bed.

Have you got cigarettes and oranges for breakfast?

I've got cigarettes and I can get oranges.

They undressed and went to bed that way with Karel who had one hand on the floor. They lay in bed smoking, their heads turning with the gin.

Julian thought: for a sexual conquest that turns out to be mutual it is not required that flattery be used by the agressor; all that is necessary is that the object feel inferior, not in intellectual qualities but in sexual attractiveness.

He changed the position of his head.

———

CHAPTER SIX: THE SAILOR

THE sun didn't shine white but the sun shone. Karel slept, loving neither flowers, animals nor music. There was no clock in the place. Louis found cigarettes and gave Julian one. Louis sat at the table and wrote with pencil on a piece of yellow paper. Julian looked at the floor strewn with cigarette butts, a broken victrola record and some glasses. An empty gin bottle stood at Louis' elbow and another lay at his ankle.

Don't you know that poems shouldn't be written after sexual excesses Julian said.

Louis said that is when I always write. He had put on Julian's dressing-gown without bothering to draw the sash together.

I suppose I'll take a bath Julian suggested if you don't mind giving me the robe. Julian looked at his face in the mirror. Before going to bed he had not removed the mascara that Karel had applied to his eyelashes and under his eyebrows was black and under his eyes was black. He applied cold cream to his face, wiped it off, and went upstairs to the tin-lined bathtub with the shower above it. The water was alternately hot and cold. Somebody had left a pair of socks in one corner. There was a bar of soap on the tub

which Julian took back downstairs. He found
Karel awake but still in bed and talking to Louis
who was dressing. Karel became quiet when
Julian entered and nothing was said until Louis,
after borrowing a book and turning his mouth
down at Karel, smiling, left, saying I'll see you
guys later.

Karel remained silent and Julian said how do
you feel?

I always feel too much but I am aware of it
Karel said.

I didn't say what do you feel.

Well, as long as I live I shall be able to extract
myself from places, sooner rather than later.

Then you cannot bear challenges? asked Julian.

Of course I meant, also dragging the spoils
with me.

I hope you will never have to commit suicide
to do that.

Karel didn't reply, considering the unexpected-
ness of his position, which had come about
inadvertently. A week ago he had looked on
Louis with intolerance and little curiosity. Louis'
way of seizing people made Karel think of a
carnivorous bird or animal. Karel saw him
hurt physically and realized the strength and
weakness of Louis whom he went to bed with.
Louis' asking was his way of taking. Karel was
filled with a sense of power because of the willingness, even eagerness, of Louis to make their

relation not a one-way affair sexually. Louis' sense of power was dilated by the fact that Karel was to keep him. Karel saw his own strength and weakness juxtaposed on that of Louis and what he saw made a whole. During the night he had just spent in bed with Julian and Louis he had heard Julian laugh and then Louis laugh and saw a segment of the whole, at the existence of which he was annoyed. He did not resent the tangent of Gabriel for he saw how he could be eliminated, in spite of Louis' having been dominated from the first by him. There were people who remembered the meeker Louis. Gabriel inspired action. Karel was sure Louis wanted to slough off Gabriel's influence not only because he feared it but also because he wanted now to show his own independence. Therefore Karel did not fear Gabriel's success if he chose to interfere, but Julian, he found, made the thing lopsided. I am moving uptown tonight he said to Julian. With Louis.

Why uptown?

I think it's safer. If I live down here Louis will get in bad with the gangsters. He's been too friendly with a few of them and they wouldn't accept his living with me. Too many undesirable people know my address anyway.

I don't guess then I'll see you very often.

You can visit us can't you?

Julian felt an absence of something he had

held dear a few minutes before. He looked around the room to see what was missing. He could find a wrong space nowhere and was sad. Then he thought he saw what he had lost. Since he saw it it must have been returned so he hadn't lost it for good.

His temporary illusion had disclosed a softness in him. A softness is a weakness and that submitted to always leaves some sort of something if only a small fear. This was a something that could be concealed by something else. He would think by what, by what it could be concealed.

Good-bye now. He looked at Karel with hard eyes and hoped the tears wouldn't come through until Karel left and when Karel left the tears didn't come through. He was learning to assume hardness. He put water and ground coffee in the pot and lit the gas. He dressed himself while thinking about love. He doubted the sincerity of the people he saw living together supposedly in love. He had never known physical and mental love towards a single person. It had always been completely one or the other. With Karel it was the other. With Louis really neither. He was unbelieving when he saw lovers who were lovers in the complete sense and who slept night after night in the same bed. He was quite sure their love was a fabrication or a convenience or a recompense and he did not believe in their love as love. There was a poem about that and he opened a book to read it and came to

'We shall say, love is no more
Than walking, smiling,
Forcing out "good morning",
And were it more it were
Fictitiousness and nothing.'
'We close our eyes, we clutch at bodies,
We wake at dream's length from each other
And love shamefully and coldly
Strangers we seem to know by memory.'
'Like dunces we still shall kiss
When graduated from music-making.'

Why had his estrangement with Karel happened
and what could Karel gain from Louis? The
coffee began to percolate and smell good. Julian
pulled the table up to the bed and sat on
the bed.

Somebody knocked coarsely from the hall.
It was Mr. Simon's Swedish boy come to sweep
and put the room in order. Sometimes he left
a pile of dirt in the middle of the floor.

Julian finished the coffee, put on his jacket,
overcoat and black hat, and went out to the street.
He was alone now for Karel was gone and he
walked along looking at the sidewalk. Little
boys with baskets of wood passed. The smell of
beer came from a basement. He would go to
the French place a few doors down and get a
'white bunny' for fifty cents, a pink drink tasting

of liquorice. He reached a door painted green and rang the bell. The lock clicked and he went in and up the steps.

The proprietor opened the door for him and he nodded once and went in. There were no other customers at that hour in the room filled with white-covered tables. The windows at the front were on a level with the elevated tracks. He sat facing them and asked for a white bunny and lit a cigarette. He sipped the drink but it was soon gone so he ordered another and waited a while before tasting it.

I hate this place which is at this moment a. lonely; b. unlovely; c. has the possibility of the same thing that anything with possibility has. And what is that but the is and the do.

He ordered another drink and that made three and four made two dollars which was all the dollars he had. He went out and down the steps. Thank God for a kind of great show and he meant by that look at them. He wasn't at home. And here *o murderpiss beautiful boys grow out of dung*.

And wear padded shoulders. They push flesh into eternity and sidestep automobiles. I bemoan them most under sheets at night when their eyes rimmed with masculinity see nothing and their lymphlips are smothered by the irondomed sky. Poor things, their genitals only peaceful when without visiting cards. They install themselves narrowly and until 11:15 their trousers must be adjusted over the exclamation point, the puritanical period that old maids prefer not to grasp although they say how *do* you do adonisprick or do they grasp it with their five-fingered wrinkled cunts. Oh they will never undress in the subway fearing imprisonment and shame. Ramon Novarro wouldn't, no, nor Richard Barthelmess and John Barrymore wouldn't though he is old enough. Harry Number wouldn't nor would Louis, no, nor Karel nor I nor the one who would like the length of it to be seen.

Their necks grow unknowingly, their eyes are eaten eventually; something explodes near their testicles and in the vicinity of their hearts (and sometimes they are nauseated). They doubtless clean spots off or out; they are soldiers without medals since they have legs with hairs on them and their heels sound. They wash themselves assuredly.

I have often imagined the curve of them next to me in bed colored like coffee or like cream or like peaches and cream powder but without peaches and cream powder in their perspiring dear pores. They have I understand eyelashes with noses to match.

I have often caught them going into toilets and coming out too.

I know the strange as it may seem pull towards the goodlooking ones, the ones with the proud rumps and the careless underlips. They have all positions but stardusters' but I wouldn't mind a starduster, at least if I could depend on him at 8:30, but a prizefighter might be better though I don't know: some movie actors have made me look for my hat extraordinarily. They should carry knives to kill those others and hang their cunts around their necks and give them to the hungry dogs. And for every one given to or stolen by them or at any rate CUT, I personally would give them each a you can guess kiss.

Wives douse them but not always; you can see them dripping yet their cuffs are clean.

Broadway is one of the streets they walk on and 72nd Street another (and there are still others o pleased to be varied God). A pair of dice would be useless: buy a pair and swallow them but sit and wait or walk and wait. Their profiles may have nothing to do with carfare, then again gin may be bought and lemons even stolen though grenadine is a luxury. All won't make love though because that's the queerest part: boys you with the bluebrown shadows among your clothes and in warm rooms the closetomeredder smell.

He turned back down Fifth Avenue because the wind was blowing and it was cold. When he reached his studio he dropped on the bed and heard for the thousandth and more time the irregular beat of his heart through his right ear on the pillow.

This did not interfere this time with how beautiful she was. She had never been so beautiful even when he was ten years old. There were violet shadows around her eyes and the nipples of her breasts were not large. She raised her arms and there was no hair under them. No hair anywhere else except the long hair from her head. She was walking by the sea and someone was coming towards her: a sailor in a blue suit with a white sailor hat on the back of his head. When she saw him she stopped and looked at him and her violet eyes with the violet shadows were gazing at him. He walked to her his body and arms swinging like they would swing a little. When he got to her he leaned on the beach with his left thigh and elbow. He was twenty years old; his name was Jack; he had green eyes and the color of his hair was the bright gold color of the short silk threads of his eyes and brow. His teeth were white like the cap he wore and his face gold to a shade as the hand he raised to her (a shade less gold than the sun's sorrow). She let her knees fall into the sand by him. She wasn't afraid of him at all, she was by the sea. They were warm to each other, he was pure. She was beautiful, it was sad to see the sailor-boy have to piss afterwards and walk away.

CHAPTER SEVEN: NAPOLEON AND THE MERRY-GO-ROUND

G ABRIEL accepted it as he might have accepted a suddenly proffered second-hand thing, unneeded and unuseful. He smiled at the Italian and put the pint of liquor in his overcoat pocket.

It was not the manner in which his lips were drawn over his teeth, or any unspoken phrase in his eyes, that, to one who was conscious of Gabriel as an entity, gave his smile the impress of derision; for if he were looked at through the eyes of a stranger his smile was acceptable enough. And often there was no lack of warmth in it—he simply did not have even a small portion of what is called charm. If it was his will to treat the lives of people objectively, hence without involving his own feelings, hence selfishly, it was his fate to be treated so by others.

He thanked the short young man with the dark suit and gray hat, buttoned his overcoat and left the speakeasy where he had spent the night and morning sitting in a chair, for he had had no room since Louis had left with Karel. He had not been drinking and had eaten no breakfast.

Walking along Fourteenth Street toward Union

4

Square, Gabriel was in one of those not so frequent days before spring when the air is cold but not penetrating, and the sun splendid and will prove to be very warming about noon if the rays of it are allowed to shine on your face and hair. He was on his way to Theodosia's where he had been going at one in the afternoon to have toast and coffee and to type Theodosia's manuscripts for which she paid him ten cents a page. Possibly two weeks he had been thus occupied. When he arrived at her apartment she was always in the bathroom, the door of which opened into the bedroom but which could be seen from the studio where Gabriel did the typing. She would crack the bathroom door an inch or two and peep at Gabriel with the announcement that she would be out in just a minute.

Gabriel had never looked into her eyes with desire. If he had considered her as an object of pleasure, it was only as a minor pleasure that could be postponed indefinitely.

When he reached the square he walked in a diagonal line to the subway entrance but did not descend the steps. Instead he walked further to the center of that tract of earth which, rumor had it, was in the process of becoming a park. Now the ground was brown and the frozen mud was softening under the heat. He stopped and looked around him: the Amalgamated Bank, Co-operative Cafeteria, S. Klein...

People picked up their legs like racehorses and walked close to the show-windows around the square. He seemed in the center of a huge merry-go-round. He looked at the sun and it blinded him for an instant. Feeling the bottle of liquor, which his hand had warmed, he took it out of his pocket and extracted the cork. Raising the bottle to his lips he tilted his head back, closing his eyes to the sun. The whisky flowed down his throat, leaving the bottle in excited regular agitations. His insides felt as if they were just being given life, as if they had had no blood before and were ready now to function. The bottle was empty and made a bright crystal twirl toward a policeman standing a mile away at the corner of Fifteenth Street and Union Square.

Gabriel must get off the merry-go-round. It was turning so fast now that it made him dizzy. It was going around and around and around and then it stopped and he almost fell over but it started again, going with more speed than ever, and his balance was regained.

He continued the diagonal line he had started and left all the men in overalls and other clothes turning in Union Square. Eighteenth Street was Theodosia. He was going to Eighteenth Street and Theodosia. He went along some street distinguished because it could exist nowhere but in a large city in the United States. He hated the people in the street as a whole and he hated them individually for he was not Napoleon that he could crush them all at once, it would have to be singly and a part of himself each time made either looser or stronger by the wound he would receive from them. He was walking along very fast and hardly swerved from a straight line so that they had to step out of his way. Something was pulling him up by the scalp and he held out his arms in readiness to grasp anything if he felt himself leaving the sidewalk. His overcoat flapped behind him. His full black kinky hair stood up like a headdress.

Eggshell is Theodosia he thought. He kept his lips shut and held in a laugh that wanted to get out. Lunatics laugh he thought and did Napoleon ever? If he laughed at Napoleon he would be a lunatic. He could feel himself laughing all over so he clamped his tongue between his teeth.

Theodosia will have just gotten out of bed. She will be in her bathroom with the charcoals of grotesque nudes on the dark green walls. She will peep out at him through the slit in the door and he mustn't curse her.

He reached Eighteenth Street and found the entrance to Theodosia's dwelling. The front door was open and he walked into the hall and back to her door which was unlocked. In the studio he shed his overcoat and fumbled with his left

hand at the knot in his tie. He took long breaths
and walked heavily towards the bathroom door.

It was opened two inches and one eye of
Theodosia looked at him. She didn't say, as
usual, just a minute. Gabriel stopped with his
lips apart and looked at the slit showing her one
eye. He was silent and seemed to be impelled
towards the thin horizontal shaft that had an eye
at the top. He was running after it (through a
tunnel) and the thing was on the end of a train
leaving him running as hard as he could; in the
darkness he stumbled, he was pitching forward
and his face would be smashed; he was falling
forward, he made no resistance and was shocked
into consciousness like if an alarm clock had gone
off. His eyes focused and it was Theodosia's
breathing close face that he saw. He felt her
arms around his neck and his arms around her
waist. He smiled sweetly as he could and
picked up her body which was taller than his
own and walked with her to the bed. She wore
a white nightgown. On the journey to the bed
she said Gabriel Gabriel and put a cheek against
his shoulder. He deposited her on the bed.
Her eyes were closed and she was breathing
rapidly. Gabriel kept his eyes on her while he
jerked off his coat for if he took his eyes away
he had a difficult time locating her again.

Theodosia had waited two weeks for this
moment. She had dreamed of it, then thought

of it, then prayed for it. Yet she had done
nothing, said nothing, ever, to show Gabriel that
she might submit to him. She had felt when
with him that her spirituality was challenged.
His thoughts seemed forever separated from the
flesh. But in her heart Theodosia desired to
make him hers just once. After that they could
ascend the mountains again—or, at least, he could.

She kept her eyes closed as she felt Gabriel
beside her. Her nightgown was being raised
and she breathed faster and faster. She felt
Gabriel's hands on her ankles and her legs slowly
bending at the knees. Oh, oh she gasped, her
eyes still closed. Then she opened her eyes
some and saw Gabriel on the bed kneeling in
front of her with his hands holding her legs
apart, his mouth descending.

Gabriel felt her faint. He was standing in the
middle of a merry-go-round and saw a nude
woman walk up behind him. She kicked his head
off. He saw his head whirl brilliantly from his
shoulders. His head was a bottle whirling in
the sun. He could see the blood gushing from
his headless trunk. It gushed like vomit.

He had vomited.

Theodosia jumped up and fled to the bathroom,
closing the door with a sob. Gabriel fell in the
place on the bed where she had lain. After a
thick voice said Napoleon, almost tenderly, he
heard nothing more.

CHAPTER EIGHT: LETTER

JULIAN,

It is not that. That wasn't the making of it. It's the unmaking. It is the unmaking of us. It is not that I am talking about: I am talking about us. About the soundless sleep at 10 a.m. with no nots for there were no yeses—only a dream and a dream is only a beginning and then we might say we were. About breakfast if quite breakfast, about walking out afterward for then we were. It is this and this I am talking about. Oh it isn't a world for scissors, for mallets; but for needle, thread and for paste: it is such a world for we were only being yes apart, not together, and that is the making of it. The making of us. Take the nights you would and I would not. That was a night and they were nights. That was when we found out about the making of it since each night was unmade usually and we were unmade and yes sometimes surely with sharp words and so we were going on. And then. There was an unmaking of it, it being we. We were not, not either, not all, not together, not apart and it is discouraging but it is good too for I am loving him, I am finding out again with someone entirely different oh so much so that there is nothing now but the writing of it. So here.

KAREL.

CHAPTER NINE: THEODOSIA

On his way to Theodosia's Julian felt that he had captured the myth and had not been captured by it.

She sat on the side of the bed with her eyes still big for him, wearing a cream-colored gown and Japanese slippers embroidered with birds. He sat in the chair and she got up from the bed and kissed his hair, forehead and eyes. The phonograph emitted music by Brahms.

I want you to live with me he said.

She went to the window and stood with her face to it.

It was bad to him that she must cry so he stood behind her and put his hands on her soft breasts.

She asked him to kiss her so he did. Kiss my breasts too she said. They were perfumed with jasmine which was sweet.

No he said.

She asked him hadn't he ever kissed a woman's breasts and he said no. She said she wanted him. I want you so much.

He wasn't frightened as he had been before and told her he hadn't any contraceptives with him. But you'll leave here today.

She told him yes she would.

I'll help you pack. Are you hungry? he **asked**. Yes she was hungry.

He went to the typewriter in the front room while she dried her eyes and dressed.

a b c d adam and eve in your own words adam pressed eve to his warmest breast and she thought whence came the fire to warm this nest whence came the bird between my breasts the red bird with the flaming crest adam told eve to lie down quietly quietly where the summer was a withheld sigh he told her to shut her eyes and not to peek and he would lie beside her and whatever came she must not arise she must not arise then to her mind came memory of the brook came memory of its chuckle and its clear fresh water and the trees that overhung the brook and that she was their daughter... but adam's hand was moving in a strange way and she must not arise and the trembling in her ankles came up to her flanks came up to her middle and the pain that still rankles broke into her mind but lying beside adam she must not arise... with eyelids pressed together tight she wondered how the clouds looked moving in the unseen skies she wondered when adam would tell her to arise but she had just as soon lie with adam this way for the pain was not so great and if he weren't so heavy she should like him to stay till the dawn bit the hill till the trees bent over saw themselves in the water with the trailing clover...

Theodosia came in and said she was ready.

Julian rolled the paper out into a wad. Where to?

Let me see...

How about the Coop?

I've never been to it.

Do you want to go?

I'll try it.

They walked there. Inside were murals showing Lenin, Marx and square bodies. The tables were filled with the usual communist crowd: young women with straight foreheads, low heels and obvious breasts; younger or older men with open or closed collars and their own hair. Some talked loudly, others listened. Julian and Theodosia had a tray each and passed beside the food on steam-tables or ice. Their selections included sauerkraut and wieners, one salami sandwich on rye bread, apple pie with whole-wheat crust and hot tea in glasses.

Theodosia saw Herbert Rector, a communist poet, sitting at a table alone. Once she had been nearly lost in the black jungles of his eyes. Let's sit with Rector she said. Julian followed her and was introduced.

Rector said he was thinking of starting a vicious, academician-smashing magazine, if he could get the capital.

But why? Julian asked him. Why should another such magazine exist after all?

Why should you exist? asked Rector.

But I'm not asking you Julian said to account for your *birth* or anyone else's. Rector looked across the other tables intensely.

They sat and ate and sometimes when Julian would not be too inconspicuous he let them know what it means not to desire being conspicuous avidly.

As to Theodosia, no other way there was to think as much as this, besides being she knew enough to know that there was some justification for her opinions in that they might not be precisely the right ones but were somewhat. She said she had finished the first act of the rewritten version of her play, *Artists and Lovers*. There is all the difference as that between a Rolls Royce and a Chevrolet in Peggy Joyce's eyes—one of them just can't be imagined she said.

What are you doing tomorrow night Julian? asked Rector and was sorry as soon as he had said it.

I'm to talk in a symposium on prose and poetry —their past difference and their modern trend in the blending.

Who invented such a subject?

Sam Slat.

You know those meetings Theodosia said of enlightenment to cellar, attic and otherwise dwellers.

Oh well Julian said and got up. The afternoon

sun is bronze and reminds me of Daddy Browning.
Bye-bye Herbert.   Theo, darling, are you coming?

They walked out, necessarily haltingly, and
went back to Theodosia's, where they put all her
books in a box, and clothes and things in two
suitcases.   The typewriter and portable phonograph also had to be taken.   After she paid the
landlady they took a taxi to Third Street and passed
Mr. Simon eating clams from a wagon on the
corner.

Theodosia seemed very happy in a troubled
way.   Julian felt so low he felt in a lower-case
mood.   If he had one thousand he thought
dollars in bills he would burn them and say I'm
an Eskimo without a jacket.   Ho hum he said.

I love something Theodosia said and sat on
the couch.   Give me a cigarette dear.

Julian lit one for her and felt her hair and said
you have a beautiful forehead.

Yes?

Yes.   *(It must be you life and poetry and
someone living uptown for me.)*   In a paramount
way of speaking he said.   He thought perhaps
an attitude of reverence and personal insuffi-
ciency might be very appropriate when considering the project of making a beautifully educated
mistress.   Anyway the charm of the perfect
effect he was creating on her must have intoxicated
him or something for he found himself kissing
her madly.   She clung to him, not unflatteringly.

Do you love me? she said. I wonder we might do so many things we might.

He picked up a copy of a review published abroad with photographs of the editor which made her look ugly as a tortoise and reminded him of the priceless photograph of dear Gertrude which was in another magazine. She looks as though she had just been hatched from a dinosaur's egg in the middle of the desert he said.

Yes Theodosia said from the heat of snakes.

Are you not perfect he said.

She told him she loved him and wouldn't they cook their own meals. And we'll work like hell too won't we darling? We'll get some things done. She said her life had been made up mostly of shocks—up to now.

Even in San Francisco?

You know that, dear.

Yes he remembered.

You were everywhere in the room: there was the chair in which you sat, the glass from which you sipped at cocktails, the cigarette stubs that had touched you. You were everywhere in the room: there were the books you opened, the air you breathed, the mood you had evoked you who went cooly.

(Emotional, yes.)

What is there to say? Looking up from my typewriter I find that the day is blue as blue as sapphires on the throats of blue-veined women.

(Did he mind her writing this? She wanted to tell him these things for he never telephoned and called once a week which was 'lots'.)

I am happy this morning. I am walking on silver and roses. I am filled with surging life. I am youth walking beneath gold stars. I am a shell filled with scarlet wine. For this, and for walking in white morning, I shall have to pay with death. I do not mind.

(Why did he misunderstand and hurt her? Well, why should she have her breasts turned always to the stars? They should have their breasts turned always to her.)

You will forget to hate me some day after. It is like crawling on one's knees on stone to an empty temple... until you turned and unclosed the blue depth beneath your eyelids... dear god... HUNGER.

(Yes, over.)

That I did not know that hunger could do this... who have known such hunger... My heart shan't burst nor my body burn to nothing nor the world crack because of this... We shall all go on but only tonight I am a white agony burning for your sake.

(He was sorry.)

I wondered if you were real or merely the image the eternal image of love staring at the mesh of moonlight staring and thinking and talking with death... Hunger for you beating at my brain like madness and weakness sucking me downward into a deep blue pool.

(He came and sat.)

It is better now I can hate you, you must not come Thursday, you must not come ever again selfish selfish person. Thank God that I so thoroughly hate you that I can't finish this.

(That wasn't all.)

And the day grows whiter in the sun's path. It means nothing. Thank God for a door and a key while under my eyelids a thousand dreams make a new ballet. Here is the place where he said so tenderly. My strange two-edged heart keeps talking. Dear God there can't be but one sin that that is to hurt, knowingly hurt, another heart.

(Wearisome and tedious is this business of mirroring the mind.)

I believe now that I will surely live until summer. This morning is beautiful and last night the cool sea wind beating the palms and grasses blew across my fevered face and I was glad. I dreamed again. I remembered dancing to Chopin's music in silver and starlight with a tragic Pierrot on whose lips were lies but whose dancing was swift music. I remembered beauty and too much laughter and always music, a perfume, a Strauss waltz, a yellow sweater-suit with small yellow suede slippers, and cafes where I dreamed, and small poems that I wrote. Eyes of men I loved. I remembered childhood and April

when I was a child, a stiffly starched little May
queen in a convent and the wind blowing the
colored ribbons.   I remembered little girls' lips
kissing me after the Maypole was wound, my face
flushed and laughing, thinking life should always
be like that.   But now I have lived too close to
death to care for anything: if that were so certain
that you could not say the word before others
for fear that they might misunderstand and pity
you, if you had to keep yourself just so, and sen-
sitised for the death that is taking you and, weak
as the body is, to above this wear a personality
and talk with people, then would you not perhaps,
having been born strange and having lived too
much, would you not gently despise the world,
and would you not if you had met someone you
loved (love being all tangled with the dream of
desire), being young in some dim corner where
death hadn't invaded yet, and if that person would
give nothing of his life, and if he did not desire
you, then, my dear, if you had so little of physical
strength, would you want it to go out in hopeless
hunger, would you not earnestly implore him not
to come back, would you not have written everything to him, that he would not come back.

CHAPTER TEN: SANTIAGO AND
MRS. DODGE

L IFE with Theodosia was much as Julian expected it to be. She was harder, more sophisticated than she had been in San Francisco. She paid the rent and her passion was not so lyrical, and he was grateful for both. What she would have called mistakes two or three years ago were now simply touches of libido. However, she was not unfaithful which may, also, have been gratifying but was nevertheless inconvenient.

He didn't have to but his mind had to. His mind had to because he wanted to. He was looking at her roaming around her body. I am you are he was. Forgive and forget are both bad words because they have grown together and thus become impossible. Beckoning is the same as becoming.

Oh I think that lovelovelovelovelovelovelove lovelovelovelovelovelovelovelovelovelovelovelove lovelovelove lovelovelovelovelovelovelovelovelove lovelovelovelovelovelovelovelovelovelovelovelove lovelovelovelovelovelovelove lovelovelovelovelove lovelove lovelovelovelovelovelovelovelovelovelove lovelovelovelovelovelovelovelovelovelovelovelove lovelovelovelovelovelovelovelovelovelovelovelove lovelovelovelovelovelovelovelovelovelovelovelove

lovelovelovelovelovelovelovelovelovelovelovelove
lovelovelovelovelovelovelovelovelovelovelovelove
lovelovelovelovelovelovelovelovelovelovelovelove
lovelovelovelovelovelovelovelovelovelovelovelove
lovelovelovelovelovelovelovelovelovelovelovelove
lllllllllllllllllllllllllllllllllllllll lllllllllllllllllllllllllllllllllllllllll
oooooooooooooooooooooooooooooooooooooooooooooo
vvvvvvvvvvvvvvvvvvvvvvvvvvvvvvvvvvvvvvvvvvvvvvv
eeeeeeeeeeeeeeeeeee eeeeeeeeeeeeeeeeeeeeeeeeeeeeeeeeee
lolololololololololololololololololololololololololo
veveveveveveveveveveveveveveveveveveveveveve
lovlovlovlovlovlovlovlovlovlovlovlovlovlovlovlov
eeeeeeeeeeeeeeeeeeeeeeeeeeeeeeeeeeeeeeeeeeeeeee
l o v e l o v e l o v e l o v e l o v e l o v e l o v e
l o v e l o v e l o v e l o v e l o v e l o v e l o v e
lxoxvxexlxoxvxexlxoxvxexlxoxvxexlxoxvxexlxoxvx
lxoxvxexlxoxvxexlxoxvxexlxoxvxexlxoxvxexlxoxvx
is grand and must be complete with Louis I wonder.

Theodosia was reading. Julian was lying on his back and heard her voice: Wyndham Lewis says that a page of a servant-girl novel smashed up equals a page of Gertrude Stein.

What Julian said Mr. Lewis means is that he thinks Miss Stein is purely negative, but he has no better word for the behavior of the organism than negative; Miss Stein is writting or walking. In one way these are the same. In neither case is she smashing the pages of a servant-girl novel.

Theodosia was pleased. Suppose we go dancing tonight at the Tavern.

I don't care.

We'll go in just a hair.   The washroom mirror showed her face with the light good on it.

Julian seldom looked at his face anymore.   Or body either, for baths made him thin.   He supposed he was still beautiful.   Gabriel told him as much the other day but Gabriel still wasn't invited to Third Street for Theodosia hated him she told Julian.   Other people too were discouraged with looks when they knocked and were admitted.   Just once, since Theodosia had moved in, a crowd gathered, about twenty people.   While they were all sitting around there was a terrible crash of glass, one of the windows; it didn't all come down and some of them rushed out and found a stone, heavy enough to kill a person, wrapped up in brown paper and on the paper was a note: DEAR JULIAN YOU'D BETTER CLOSE UP THE PLACE BEFORE IT'S TOO LATE WE'RE SORRY FOR THE LADY BUT.   Some had their arms in their coats and were persuaded to stay.   No more stones came in.   Frederick Spitzberger was there and after he had recited a poem, a communist, rather innocent looking with short arms and everything else short perhaps for that matter, got up and started without equivocation and with much authority in his tone to talk about poetry as a secondary sexual characteristic; in other words that poets write to attract the opposite sex or some sex and as he went on one of the things he said six times, for he was long on repetition, was that poetry began when women started to menstruate (which rather upset Theodosia). Everybody expected Frederick or Julian to get up and say something and so Julian did but they thought him much too human. He was solemn about it and pointed out how he was sure it was his envy of the social confidence of poets that had caused the young man to speak, and that it was his communistic frustration, an inability to find the proper social outlet, that had caused him to envy something that seemed successful and yet which he had to condemn as inferior because such talent was entirely denied him. Julian said communists *regret* anything definite, they are all so hazy. Then the young man got up and started talking again and after admitting he hadn't really been serious in many things he said, which was a lie Julian thought, he dragged out a lot of facts and too familiar and accepted theories and then Frederick got up and intoned at him you are the type whose seriousness is its one vice. Do you think we are unacquainted with all these *clichés* you've been divulging and what do you propose to do about the dreadful situation that there are women who don't parturite and men who fail to produce intellectual progeny. In answer to this he said tell the women to be normal and stick to what they're good for and everybody howled. So Julian got up again and almost

yelled for Christ's sake is that all you can do
become excited over a number of facts you haven't
any idea how to readjust?... Since then there
had been no more meetings.

Theodosia came from the washroom.

Shall we have something to drink first? Julian
asked.

Yes let's go to Frankie's.

What about the French place?

It's cheaper at Frankie's and they have a radio.

That doesn't help the depressing air of the
dump Julian said. He helped Theodosia with
her coat and put on his own.

They crossed Macdougal Street and saw Gabriel
who didn't say hello. Steps led down into the
big basement of Frankie's, a place of dim lights,
bare walls, and a floor scattered thinly with
sawdust. Four people played cards at a corner
table. Theodosia knew one of them, a poet who
once captivated her with his voice loving sonnets
by Cummings; because he played cards with
the customers at Frankie's he got his drinks free.
Julian and Theodosia sat at a table by the opposite
wall. They ordered white wine, which Julian
paid for, fifteen cents a glass, with money Theodosia had given him. They had two more glasses
apiece and were on their fourth when Vivian
came in. She was alone and looked very young.
She stood in the doorway until her eyes hit Julian,
then slowly and stiffly, with one elbow bent, she

walked to his table. Her smile looked as if it had been attached. She said softly hello and Julian said hello.

You are not so beautiful now but you are still beautiful she said, standing by the table. Theodosia took a sip of wine and looked at her.

Yes? Julian said and smiled.

She said yes and walked archly and slowly, with the cocaine in her, to the table where the card game was going on.

The wine had been paid for in advance so they got up and climbed the steps out of there.

When they entered the Tavern Santiago was dancing the whip dance in a red light. Rose came up shushing and pointed to a table with seats for them. It was crowded.

Quite a few from the busses tonight Julian said to Rose.

Listen our customers are not from the busses she said.

Julian saw K-Y and Windward, also Osbert with his lips hanging at Santiago's dancing. Word was going around that this was Santiago's last night at the Tavern because Rose said People were beginning to Talk. His whip dance went a little too far as a demonstration. Of course Rose didn't *know*, but it looked to her (and others) as if sex played too large a part in it, considering the expression on his face and his exhaustion (momentary) at the end of it. Julian liked the dance—the way the whip cracked and his heels clicked and one hand caressed his oiled curly black hair. Rose was a dolt. But it embarrassed some not to applaud.

The negro at the piano played next for everyone to dance but the floor was too small for everyone at once. Julian and Theodosia danced together.

Santiago was sitting by K-Y and Windward said to him you frighten me. Santiago asked him if he had ever tried the Mammoth Caves... It was long enough after K-Y's abortion for her to drink so she was drunk. She was looking at Theodosia. Do you all want a drink? she called to Julian.

We'll see you after this piece Julian said.

You're damn right K-Y said.

When they were together Julian was sitting by Santiago and Theodosia next to K-Y. Rose came over and told them they were making too much noise and that two Russians of the aristocracy wanted to meet Julian and his dancing partner. Julian was not interested but Rose insisted and got him to get up with Theodosia.

Come back you hear K-Y said.

The Russians were very polite and gave them *chartreuse* to drink and they ate chicken sandwiches and drank gingerale with them. They wanted to know could Julian and Theodosia join them after 3 a.m. and go to another place to drink. Julian said thank you we'll see.

The piano man was playing.

Julian said you will excuse us. He danced again with Theodosia. When they were by Windward's table K-Y told them to sit down and have a drink.

What have you got?

Harlem rye. K-Y insisted that they sit down.

Mrs. Dodge with dark purple eyelids had joined the group, blinding everyone with the neck of her dress, a wide band of brilliants. She was laughing loud at Santiago who had just asked her if she had ever done anything with her breasts besides let them hang. He means have you ever had it between them Julian said. She liked Julian very much.

Osbert was in a corner booth, angry and drunk. After a minute he got up and went out. Mrs. Dodge looked at Santiago.

Let him go Santiago said. He bores me when he's drunk.

K-Y, while pouring drinks for everyone, was talking close to Theodosia's ear and Theodosia was fascinated.

Windward was thinking why wasn't he in Harlem for he loved beautiful negresses.

Jesus I'll be wild drunk mixing drinks Julian said.

No you won't darling Mrs. Dodge said. I'll take care of you.

I'll take care of him Santiago said. That's my charm.

Windward, feeling that he was being ignored, took the pint bottle from under the table and drank from it the rest of the contents. Then he flung it towards the pianist's back and it crashed against his head, scattering all over the dance floor.

K-Y screamed and people screeched and talked and Rose rushed over belching and the place was in a hubbub. Many were leaving and a small mob was in front of the hat-check window.

Julian was separated from the others and he was in it. He meant people and politics and awful ideas and people and muscles and chastity and fear and people and print and sometimes he felt as though he could do without the people. When he was finally on the sidewalk outside with his coat and hat he saw K-Y and Theodosia together, saw them jump into a taxicab and leave. Windward was not in sight.

Mrs. Dodge and Santiago emerged and came up to Julian and Santiago said where shall we finish it?

Julian said come to my place there's some gin.

Mrs. Dodge hailed a taxi and the three got in. When they reached Third Street she paid the driver while Julian unlocked the door to the studio.

Come on in and undress he said.

Mrs. Dodge said please and Santiago took off his blouse.

Julian put a bottle half full of gin on the table and said goddamn her.

Ah ha Mrs. Dodge laughed.

You all sleep here Julian said.

Mrs. Dodge took off her clothes. She was short and fat and glowing. All three were nude. They got in bed, Julian between them.

You're the only sissy I ever loved Santiago said to him. He's the only sissy I ever loved Santiago said to Mrs. Dodge. He put his arm around Julian who moved closer to Mrs. Dodge. Damn you he said and hit Julian, but not hard, on the top of the head.

Be nice Mrs. Dodge said.

Julian's eyes and lips were closed.

Be nice now.

Santiago got out of bed and poured himself a drink. He went in the kitchenette for some water. He came out with a glassful and dashed it in Julian's face.

Julian didn't move.

Don't be a stinker Mrs. Dodge said to Santiago.

I'm leaving he answered. He put his boots and blouse on and slammed the door behind him.

But you are aren't you? Mrs. Dodge asked Julian. But you are aren't you? but you are aren't you?

CHAPTER ELEVEN : LOVE AND JUMP BACK

THEODOSIA returned the next day. After she had stacked her things in a taxi, after much crying, after blue and brutal words and no kisses, she left. Julian was surprised that he should feel pain about it because he had felt joy at what he had decided to have happen. So he stood by the door that dropped to the sidewalk. Then she could see him standing there and looking at her as she drove away with her love wetting her handkerchief. He stood with a drained face, his hands behind him on the doorknob, and said good-bye. It didn't exist any more if it had ever existed and a quick over was better.

Oh damn you good-bye Theodosia cried and beat one hand on the glass behind the taxidriver for him to go; with the other hand she put her handkerchief to her nose.

Julian shivered and went back inside. He found a cigarette butt and lit it. Theodosia had been thoughtful and for a time not *gauche*. He felt hollow in his stomach. He must hurry.

Through Gabriel he had learned that Karel and Louis had moved from 49th Street down to 14th Street. He even knew the number on 14th

Street and he must hurry for he felt a hollow place in his stomach. When will my soul arise and say to me now aren't you glad you've kept me all these years. That is will it ever. If only I had been born as ugly as Bernard Shaw or as old as Thomas Hardy then there would have been no alternative: I should have *had* to be a genius.

He walked along Fifth Avenue and thought if he should really meet, actually MEET President Hoover on his way he would say, oh well what would he say except: I am what I am and I would for the price of a suit and overcoat and would you throw in a hat, please, Mr. Hoover?

He was going mad he firmly believed. Even in Paris and Berlin he thought there would be repetitions. Was he beginning to decay or what? His blood he felt was many engines; his heart was chasing them.

At the number on 14th Street he turned into an unlighted hall and stairs with the carpet gone. He looked at the names by the telephone and found they lived in room eleven. At the turn of the staircase stood a chair of almost antique workmanship which he didn't feel tired enough to sit in.

He knocked on door 11. No one answered. Knocking again he said Karel,—Louis,—it's Julian, open up. He heard the bed squeak and the bolt slide back; the door opened; the lights were on. My God he said walking in, with this wallpaper one couldn't *help* thinking of Shelley.

Karel had opened the door for him. He looked at Karel and wondered how long since he had combed his hair and saw that his eyebrows looked neglected too.

Take your coat off and sit down Karel said unsurprisedly. He has the balls of his eyes left Julian thought iris pupil and all but what has happened to his eyelashes?

Louis, who was sitting by the table with note-book and pencil, didn't acknowledge him. His hair was almost as long as Karel's but it was coarser. He threw his smoking cigarette on the floor and stepped on it.

Julian said I'll keep my coat on I'm here just for a minute.

Theo, where is she? Karel asked.

Why shouldn't he have heard about the beginning if not the end. I don't know. I'm not living with anyone now.

Things do become don't they Karel said.

Louis got up and looking at Karel said I'm going out for coffee.

Remember that's our last fifty cents until I get a check from the *Post* Karel said.

He's a monster I couldn't possibly worship thought Julian.

Louis asked him if he didn't know by this time that he got coffee when he wanted it. He picked up his overcoat.

Wait a minute said Julian give me a cigarette.
Louis gave him one of the two left.

Are you keeping up with your rent here?

We've been in this room part of the week and
owe for half of it in advance Karel said.

Don't worry about the rent said Louis I've
got an idea.

So have I Julian said; why don't you all move in
with me? You can have the bed on the floor and
I'll take the one on the balcony. We'll each pay
a third of the rent. It won't be much.

Karel looked at Louis and then at Julian.

I don't care Louis said.

Karel raised his shoulders and his underlip,
then let the shoulders fall.

We'll get out now Louis said and take this
mirror. There was a long mirror on the wall
above the washbowl.

No, no said Karel.

Sure, we'll take the fucking mirror.

Why not the mattress? asked Julian.

Leave the mattress Louis said.

And the mirror. Pack what you have to pack
and leave with me. Now Julian said.

Karel pulled his two battered suitcases from
under the peeling white-enameled bed. They
contained old manuscripts and a few dirty clothes.
He added some books and toilet articles and that
was all.

They walked down the steps, making as little

noise as possible. The landlady lived on the floor above; she was caught peeping through the keyhole on the second night of their stay and this gave them an advantage; hence the balance due on the rent.

Louis wanted to take the ancient chair to sell it but they wouldn't assist him. Outside he said let's get a taxi.

But—

He raised his hand for one and they rode to Third Street; he gave the half-dollar to the driver. In the studio he continued on a poem he was writing when Julian intruded.

Karel had been reading Cummings' play which he had seen at the Provincetown theater. He took the book from one of the suitcases. The most important event in American literary history of the last decade he said is the fact that *Him* was produced a few hundred yards from Washington Arch, New York City.

Louis closed his notebook and said Cummings is the only comic poet America has ever had. He's made underdone meat seem tender.

Julian was making coffee behind the partition. America doesn't know how to be comic he called; it knows only how to be Freudian. He was thinking anyway he might like Louis if he didn't like Karel better.

When the coffee was strong enough to drink someone knocked. Louis guessed the place was popular as ever.

It's only beginning Karel said going to the door and opening it when he saw Herbert Rector outside.

Greetings were given and Herbert wanted to know what Karel was doing that night besides composing effeminate poetry.

I shall write an open letter to you and send it to the *New Masses* Karel told him.

Is that so? How about speaking in a symposium, the three of you, on political liberty and the artist?

Where?

At the Round Table. I'm chairman. How about it?

Julian demurred, being more timid than he appeared.

Louis said he wouldn't speak without a fee but why don't you speak Karel?

You'd let a cow's tongue lick your ass for a fee wouldn't you? Herbert remarked to Louis.

I might speak said Karel.

O. K. Be there not later than nine. I'll depend on you.

Very well.

Julian invited him to have coffee with them but he declined with a gesture and left.

I am waiting for the day Louis said when I can destroy all definitions.

But until then said Karel they are the most that matters.

I think I'll write a novel tonight Louis said. I could write it in one night and sell it tomorrow.

Yes Julian said this is an age in which talent is readily encouraged and unwise talent corrupts the economic situation... Which is the worse, physical or spiritual suffering?

Physical is the most immediately intolerable Louis said.

Karel started typing his paper for the symposium.

Louis said don't you know the dopes that go to the Round Table are looking more for social than intellectual stimulation?

Yes Karel told him but I want to find out if by now I'll be neglected as a spectacle; and don't *think* it will be a naive one.

There's hardly a demand for spectacles in America now. There's a demand for nothing but reassurance.

It was beginning to be dark inside so the candle on the table was lighted and the amber globes turned on. Karel, sitting on the couch, typed by the floor light.

Everyone was silent until he finished typing; then the covered glass on the door was tapped and Julian looked out. He saw a fat man wearing a derby. The man nodded without speaking. Julian didn't know him. Who in God's name is this he said letting the curtain fall and telling Karel to look.

What! Karel was excited and said he would see. He had put on a dressingrobe and his hair was disordered and covered his ears. He looked at the man, who had tapped again as soon as Julian dropped the curtain back. Karel didn't know him either. The man raised his hat politely and said through the glass may I come in madam?

This isn't a tea-room Karel said and covered the window. There was more tapping.

Let me take a look at him. Louis went to the window. What the hell do you want? Louis saw him take a gallon jug of wine from under his coat.

Let me in. I won't stay long he pleaded.

Let's let the sap in Louis turned to them. He's got a whole gallon of wine.

Karel protested but Julian said it was all right with him.

He was admitted, looking and puffing.

Please! Julian said and decided to drink as much wine as he wanted. Take off your drags dear. What's your name?

I'm an old son-of-a-bitch.

Karel covered his ears.

Louis wrinkled his eyes and said let's have some wine and reached for the jug.

Stop I'm taking this home to my childless mother. For medicinal purposes. He was serious and completely ugly.

You wouldn't be mean would you? said Julian

and touched his double chin. The man's hand strayed and Julian jumped back. Stop you bastard.

That's right. Call me a bastard please. I'm a son-of-a-bitch!

Julian fetched glasses from the kitchenette. Here pour us some wine, Annie.

He poured out four glasses almost full. There. He toddled over to the couch hugging the jug which was placed between his feet. He looked like the president of a Merchants & Farmers Bank. Come sit down he said holding out a fat hand to Karel.

Kiss my foot! said Karel, pointing his toe.

Call me a son-of-a-bitch.

You son-of-a-bitch!

They all tittered except the guest who seemed content enough. Contented people don't laugh.

Give us some more wine Julian said holding out his glass.

For a kiss, my dear.

Degenerate! Julian said. Pour the wine first. His glass was refilled carefully.

I want some too! Karel stamped his foot.

No.

Karel gave him a light slap on the head. Give me some! His glass was filled again.

Louis extended a glass asking if he was to be left out.

Here. That's all you can have.

Louis said to the health of him.

To universal castration said Julian.

Karel said to beauty, thy name is too good to be true. He went to the washroom to apply a little powder, followed by the old man who forgot to pick up the jug. Julian made for it, poured himself and Louis a glass each and left refilled Karel's glass on the chest of drawers.

Karel stumbled out with the man behind him. I've been insulted. He turned to his would-be seducer. Listen fuck-mouth keep your hands off me unless you intend to marry me.

I'm leaving. His suitor was contrite.

What a mess-face you turned out to be. Julian and Louis were tickled. Get on out then and next time you come bring fifty dollars. Julian helped him with his coat and jug.

Bye-bye now.

He went.

How sickening fools are sickening!

What putridity.

The time the time.

Almost nine.

You two are coming aren't you?

Julian said he might as well that beggars can whistle.

It's late said Louis.

It may be a little late for friends but it's never too late to destroy your enemies. I know just what I'm going to say.

We haven't eaten Louis said.

There'll be sandwiches and coffee.

Julian with wine was ready for any place except bed by himself. Get ready and let's fly.

They entered the Round Table just as Rector was announcing the second speaker in the symposium.

Julian saw Gabriel at a table with Frederick. Karel didn't want to sit with Gabriel but Frederick screamed for them all to come over so they went.

There was a crowd.

The speaker was interrupted several times by the sound of Frederick's voice whispering things in a tone that carried to Karel or Julian. When he was through he glared at Frederick who was accustomed to being glared at. Frederick had been reciting an incident that happened on the subway that evening; he was sitting with his usual acquired aristocratic dignity and gradually became aware of the adjacent woman staring at him, how long she had been staring he didn't know. He turned to her and said why how do you do, you look *so* much worse since your accident. What do you mean? she said. You *must* have been in an accident to have a mug like that Frederick said. I'LL SLAP YOUR FACE YOUR DEPRAVED THING YOU came from the woman in a loud hysterical voice. Frederick had turned his eyes away and tried not to notice the agitation among the other passengers.

Rector announced that Karel was the next speaker and Karel got up. He began:

I am glad, in a way, that I was asked to contribute to this symposium on political freedom, because it struck me when I was asked, first of all: I did not have anything to say on the subject; and then: I might have something to say, for after all political reality may govern more of each of us than most of us take the trouble to consider— I mean of course that politics, which is socially determined, may have more effect on our personal lives than we give its civic, state and national agents credit for—and by 'we' I mean those of us who have felt that a personal life, intelligently conducted from within, is about the most that may be done for the individual...

Will you have this light cut out Mr. Chairman it's shining in my eyes... thank you.

The adorable Kareletta Frederick giggled.

He continued:

On the face of it, I am not concerned one way or the other about political freedom, because I have been accustomed to think of myself as an individual and not as a member of the mass of society. I feel that I am as 'free', in the ethical sense, as the limitations (that is, the inherent limitations) of the individual permit me to be. I can never govern myself perfectly, because I am a mechanism full of defects, and when I do not think of myself as a mechanism, I am aware of my inability to reach the ideal state of spiritual serenity.

Frederick wondered to Julian where Karel's feather fan was.

However, the idea of political freedom must open for anyone the vista of a kind of Utopian existence, where one is free because his fellows are also free. We realize of course that political freedom for the mass and therefore for the individual signifies in theory the official power of the mass of the people to control its social destiny, presumably with more satisfaction than the existent system of government provides.

Of course, this is familiar ground, because we all know what the minor political parties such as the communists and the socialists are fighting for: a new system of government, and, as I have just explained, the obvious interpretation which we give the phrase, political freedom, is the right accorded by legislature to the mass of the people to govern itself—that is, to see that it is governed in a superior manner than that in which it is now governed.

I said at the beginning that the reason my second thought prompted me to say something on this subject is that, notwithstanding the way this phrase was intentionally put tonight, or may be put at any time, it may be interpreted to mean something more immediately significant to every individual—strange as it may seem—and I come to a conclusion different from what my impulse intended.

Now before going any further I want to say that I don't doubt for a moment that the economic handicap, which communism proposes to dispel, is a very important one—it is above all important to such as I am, the artist, who, if he is really an artist and is not especially lucky, leads a hand to mouth existence. I even grant that a successful application of some new theory of government may relieve nearly all the civilized world of what is known as the economic burden. I even grant that this theory might be communism, when it has come to be understood and not reviled by rabid prejudice.

BUT—I am convinced that for most of us—for all of us I may say who are aware of the possession of a soul—the secret of political freedom does *not* lie in the removal of our economic difficulties.

Thus, I posit that man is not concerned primarily with the conceptual realization of his material welfare but with the conceptual realization of his spiritual welfare. Accordingly we may reason that it is when a man feels most like a well-fed pig that his spiritual responsibilities should occur to him with the most force. Perhaps to some of you this idea of spiritual responsibility may seem almost comic if you have had the ill fortune as I have had to go hungry for a day;

at such a time the solution to all enigmas seems a thoroughly good meal...

(Applause from a run-down looking individual in the rear.)

...but upon reflection this notion will be found to be childish—

(Laughter and necks craning at the abashed applauder.)

The artist, whose mental activity goes at a greater rate of speed than the mental activity of anyone else, finds absent meals, bedless nights and overcoatless cold are merely incidental; he can think just as sharply and rapidly in a cold doorway as he can in a steamheated room after a heavy meal—in fact, if his physical being is thoroughly comfortable he *may* be inclined to nap rather than to think. I don't think any artist, at bottom, resents his past unhappiness in the material world; his critic's sense of detachment saves him from such a nostalgia. What the artist may resent is the pettiness of other men, who cannot realize that at a very minimum sum all his needs may be taken care of—and still the affluent man, through his stupidity or selfishness, withholds this sum. Yet this resentment that the artist holds is momentary; it is the result of a circumstantial thing which will not, in the last resolution of experience, affect his work, if he has a pound of good luck.

I cite the artist's attitude to show merely that

any acute man will reason that activity is the secret of accomplishment—to speak vulgarly: if we do not move, we will not get anywhere; and, at least, when we are in physical want, action becomes assured, because it is necessary.

Any artist, of course, prefers leisure to a routine of eight hours a day, the absence of which is leisure to him. All of us, in fact, prefer leisure. But the work of the world must go on. It is really, to the ordinary person, his economic obligation, which he cannot escape in some way, which chains him to an uninteresting reality. Therefore, while this dull part of life forms an inevitable part of his being, it is to his spiritual nature to which he is compelled to turn for a refreshment of his interest in life—hence his enormous attendance at the movies and his excursions to amusement parks on Sunday.

To the ordinary person, then, political freedom may mean in pretty accurate substance an economic serenity which will give him a comfortable home, money to go to the movies every night, to go to Coney Island on Sunday, to buy a radio, and even a fur coat if such his heart desires.

But to the slightly above the average person, the means for the satisfaction of his desires are more complicated, because his desires are more complicated and potential. Political freedom for this person signifies his lonely braving of contrary spiritual elements, his gauntlet-down challenges to ideas, which may be friendly or inimical, life-giving or deadly...

Indeed, *this* sort of political freedom is the sort for which relatively few of us are really prepared.

Karel went back to his table. There was some applause around.

Whatever occurred after you closed your lips on the last syllable certainly throttled Gabriel said.

Well I pointed out some things that shouldn't be lost to the immediate public said Karel.

Julian turned to Gabriel saying do you know I could live in a world with only vision?

Gabriel said if I really do something dreadful in the way of living that is for my contemporaries.

A young Jew came panting over to Karel and said he must have the honor to meet personally one whose work he so admired and wouldn't he tell a few things about himself?

Well Karel said I contribute to magazines and you can get some of them at Brentano's. He would have liked to have said other things but just then Herbert reproved them for talking and since there was no more room at the table he didn't speak to the poor dear again.

After so long a time the speakers were through and coffee and sandwiches were welcomed by most.

It was sad to Frederick as it was to Julian to see that Karel's appearance was not what it used to be. But Karel was thinking of Louis turning queer so beautifully gradually and beautifully like a chameleon like a chameleon beautifully and gradually turning.

All women are fugitives Gabriel said and washed his mouth with a big drink of coffee. That is why they are fundamentally more conscious of time than men are.

All writers must have at least one fugitive piece Julian said. He looked at Gabriel's meeting in the center eyebrows and the eyes beneath were as beautiful as ever before. A man cannot want a woman and a woman cannot want a man he thought not really. He thought so looking at Gabriel.

Gabriel turned away, only his head and shoulders some. Who was in flight, was it he? Karel asked himself. Yes, he wanted to evade Gabriel and any obligation to him.

Strung along the walls were some of Osbert's paintings. Louis felt called upon to comment on them. Painting he said is blasé, disingenuous, and defensive; photography is pure wonder.

He must always be commenting on something Julian thought.

That puts too great a responsibility on the photographer Karel said. He must be himself after all.

That's cowardly Gabriel said.

You're safe anyway Louis Frederick chimed. You're not a photographer are you?

You guys ought to start taking pictures Louis answered. Photograph each other. Julian take a photograph of Frederick and Gabriel like this— but Frederick evaded the posture and said it's quite possible to faint when you chew something up. He took a piece of cheese sandwich between his teeth.

Do you feel that you have been cheated of anything in life? Gabriel asked him.

You mean feel that I have been deprived of something, denied it at birth?

Yes, or perhaps something may have happened which changed your life, something that you regret.

Well Frederick said then I may say that I have been cheated of WINGS.

I don't know how important they might be Julian said.

I don't know how important poetry is said Karel.

Poetry may have no scale of recognizable value Louis said.

In other words, it may be valuable simply as form, good or bad? from Julian.

Yes Louis said only poetry, the thing, has value and that is continuous; therefore only poetry has complete logical existence; poems are incomplete and illogical.

I don't agree with you Karel said.

Nor do I Julian said.

Louis is right said Gabriel. Poetry is the expression of a continuous state of being.

I suppose connected in some way with cosmology said Frederick.

If this were true Karel said images in poetry would be deprived of their validity; sound would render a phrase rather than a harmony—for the ultimate value of any particular experience or any of its parts would have to be related to a whole which could be communicated only by an *extra-artistic* technique.

In other words Louis said by an abstraction.

Yes obviously poetry is not a shadow Frederick put in.

It is rather the thing which casts shadows Karel finished.

Someone turned the radio on full blast just as Louis opened his mouth so he saved what he was going to say.

Frederick leaned over to the adjoining table and said much soap is wasted by being left on the shaving brush. The two Columbia girl students thought he was crazy and made ready to leave.

Julian went to tone down the radio and heard Karel say words are ugly and are innately regarded by men as such, but they are necessary therefore they are called beautiful. He loved Karel, he wanted him for himself, he hated Louis. But he wondered did he love him for Karel's self or an idea Karel represented; but can anyone be loved any other way?

The longer I live in the world the more I'm convinced that Christ was the most important madman we've had Frederick said and made a terrible face. He got up to go. When will you be at home? he asked Karel.

I don't know Frederick you'd better phone any time before you come. That was being mean but guardful. If Frederick was 100 % positive he was desirable in a room as a guest only 50 % of the time he was in the room as a guest. Karel considered this.

Frederick asked him if he were going to the drag on Saturday of next week.

No said Karel I'm not.

Julian said I'm going.

Are you darling. Then we'll go together. I must do something septic to boredom. At my age I've learned that wickedness is its own reward. All right. I'll see you at your dwelling. Good-bye said Frederick.

Good-bye.

Good night.

Money is the one indomitable value Gabriel said. The most perfect and complete thing a person can be is a charge on the community.

That is society to the point of retching Louis said.

Is it? asked Julian and is it? asked Karel, their eyes blooming like four daisies.

Julian turned to Karel asking him what he was going to do. Karel didn't know, he supposed he would go back.

Don't go back Julian said. Let's do something like getting a bottle of wine and something else nice and—

No Karel was interested enough in going to the place with Louis.

You can go there later. We'll go back together. Come on with me now will you Julian said.

Go ahead you can meet me later—let me have the key Louis said to Karel.

But I don't want to said Karel I'm not going to.

Julian thought no more of it and felt that defeat would be something he would never want to know anything about. He looked at Gabriel and said let's take a walk.

Gabriel was willing.

They left Karel and Louis sitting at the table. Walking along they stepped over puddles for it had been raining. It was so heavy and black the sky was. Like Gabriel's hair or the heart of Julian if he would look at it, a young heart. Gabriel was the shorter and imitated the straight from side to side walk, the inconspicuous left-right balance-turn-on-either-foot of the gangsters. It was a walk that wearied the spectator because it was so deliberate. It liked itself to Julian sometimes because it was ape-like.

I admire the way you hold your head and

shoulders when you walk Gabriel said to Julian unexpectedly.

Julian said where are we going? It is one o'clock again. Where ah where oh where. Where? Where.

There's a house-warming party that we could crash said Gabriel.

Julian said no.

We might drop in on Theo.

Where is she living now?

The first place she had before she went with you.

I wouldn't think of going there. Especially at this hour. Have you been to see her. Lately?

Once. She asked who it was through the door and wouldn't let me in.

Vincent and Tony may be at home.

Not those said Gabriel.

How about Harold's?

Not the subway.

Then we'll have coffee and decide. We'll make a decision said Julian and led the way into a coffee pot. They sat on stools. It was, Julian could if he wanted to remember, the coffee pot where he first met Gabriel and Louis. It seemed a long time ago to him.

They ordered coffee but before they had time to sweeten it a man sitting at a table up the aisle threw off his shirt and was unbuttoning his trousers. He was undressing. The one lady customer with her gentleman friend just had time to fly when his trousers were pulled off and there he stood. Then he sat. Not a bad sight thought Julian. His shoes came off and Julian was about ready to burst.

The people who run this place are too complacent Gabriel said.

The waiters were standing with their fingers on either side of their semi-white aprons over their hips.

Julian didn't dare look any more and said ohwo wo oohw.

Gabriel said he couldn't be drunk he must be mad.

He came down the aisle toward them. Two men across the way were just leaving. Into the vacated chair of one of them he threw his pants and said *there y' are cap*! and money or keys jangled in them. Gabriel and Julian hadn't any more than averted their eyes when a tall policeman came in and made a bee line toward the doubtless maniac. A huge crowd was looking in.

Julian who had meantime consumed three-fourths of his cup of coffee said let's go.

By all means said Gabriel and gulped his coffee down.

If we can do so with dignity said Julian leaving the change on the counter.

They heard the policeman ask DO YOU WANT TO GO TO BELLEVUE WHAT DAY OF THE WEEK IS IT DO YOU

WANT A NICE LITTLE RIDE HUH?

Julian and Gabriel were right in the window and were only obstructing the view and they supposed they might be thought to be accomplices so they moved on.

Julian liked to drink, even on his last money. A few of his books were left. Those that had not been taken he had sold since Theodosia. He had money in his pocket and asked Gabriel if he would like to get some wine or a pint of gin.

Gabriel said he didn't want any. Have you any more cigarettes? Go ahead and drink if you want.

He wouldn't drink unless Gabriel wanted to he thought once and thinking twice he thought he would but not back at the place so where. Single drinks at a bar were too much. Go with me to the restaurant on Barrow, the Italian one. I'll get two pint bottles of wine and maybe you'll have some.

O. K.

When they got there Gabriel waited on the curb.

The bell having been rung the Italian woman admitted Julian into the hall. He told her a quart of wine in two pints and looked at himself in the mirror while she went to the rear for it.

One of the pints he gave Gabriel to carry; the other he put in the pocket of his own overcoat. To go back to Third Street would be perhaps to find thirsty throats. They had better stop in dark doorways. Julian lit a cigarette for a chaser. Gabriel wouldn't drink. Julian took half of the wine in the bottle he held. A taste for bad wine may be cultivated like sexual perversions and any number of other dubious refinements. This fact Julian thought he had discovered hiding like a rabbit. Gabriel watched him drink more wine in other doorways but Julian couldn't tell whether Gabriel was amused or not. It was Julian's naïveté: having to have a sum of actions and reactions before he could make a subtraction. The last entrance had a dim light in it. Gabriel took his first and last sip from the second bottle and Julian finished it and felt like beauty. He couldn't know if he looked it but Gabriel touched Julian's ear and would have kissed him flatly on the mouth but Julian didn't want his mouth kissed by Gabriel. You're my *intellectual* lover! Julian told him and ventured to kiss his forehead. If I should die before I take I pray the Lord my soul to wake. He was with Gabriel because he wasn't with Karel. A few leaves to be eaten before the little root included Gabriel. Or the root might include Gabriel if it should not be bitter enough. Are you hungry Gabriel?

He wasn't particularly hungry.

Are you tired and hungry?

Hunger, like isolation, is a habit Gabriel said.

They were walking on uncrowded streets. Once the contents of a taxicab argued in front of a rooming house. Everything as a whole was entirely too peaceful. As they approached West Broadway Gabriel said I was standing here a week ago tonight when a woman drove an automobile by and called out 'There's a dead man on the corner!'

Gabriel didn't care Julian thought (the wine he knew had made him as drunk as it would make him) whether he was believed or not. Surely this is a calm world he said though a strange, strange one; one that ought to be less strange than it is, everything considered.

Gabriel knew that no planets need be pushed out of the way for them, nor need the laws of the constitution be revised in order for himself to practise abstinence and even rigor. Hearts other than their own needed to be emptied for them to be refilled and other haunches belabored not by themselves and aplenty.

Julian looked in through the plateglass windows of one after another cafeteria. They went in a corner one and took green tickets from an upright box that rang a bell when a ticket was taken and it was a precious thing there because if you lost one it had to be found.

What do you want? said Julian. Take some scrambled eggs.

Scrambled eggs said Gabriel. The waiter who took their order looked like a Hungarian.

Make it two Julian said and almost posed.

He might decide to kiss Gabriel even, later.

Coffee? asked the little one who was also muscular.

Two coffees!

They picked up their eggs and coffee and sat at a table near the front, Julian with his back to the cashier so he could observe the service.

Gabriel could not talk and eat too so Julian ate without saying a word other than I feel good.

Gabriel washed the last of his eggs down with coffee and said monotony is man's passion; diversion is his excuse for failure in that passion.

What is divine besides slang Julian wanted to know. I mean there are other things that are divine.

Tip the velvet.

I won't ask you what that means. It has the implications of the centuries.

One immortal saying of this century is Cummings': (poetry) competes with elephants and El Greco.

Julian put both elbows on the table and said I am going through a startling series of transpositions.

Gabriel turned his eyes on him. Fiction versus poetry? Love concept versus love concept? Behavior versus concept?

I must, it seems, love not people alone but people as ideas.

You are not Joan of Arc said Gabriel.

The only thing that consoles me is, well I

really feel like Cinderella. You know. I'm just in that mood.

Gabriel said if you think I don't feel venomous toward everybody you're wrong. For instance, can I help it if Ernest Hemingway cannot write over my head and thus has one admirer less?

I approve of him Julian said but only because he sits on Sherwood Anderson's right hand as well as he can.

When I think of the people in the world, all of them, I begin to get saintly said Gabriel. I mean such as those who sit at tables next to you in restaurants and actually eat.

What about literature, the baggage now?

To hell with it. I don't wonder that it fails so often when people like William Rose Benet, Henry S. Canby and Amy Lowell take it up.

Oh well Julian said a lot of fairly good work is being done presently.

But I wouldn't take all of twentieth century poetry for *Romeo and Juliet*. The point is that everyone must have jobs and there are 99 competent milliners to one creative artist.

But people are so nice and lovely and ridiculous and monstrous and America is so Greek but doesn't know it.

To hell with Greece Gabriel continued as smug as pugnosed Socrates with his platonic carryings on.

It's easy to discover literature said Julian.

Yes but how about the time and space that Shakespeare wrestled with, his muscles standing out marvelously! Gabriel got up to get a glass of water.

Julian looked at his back and sleeves and thought I shall write more beautiful than ever poetry when I can find someone who yes I cannot live like this without lovers without them because I am not at all ambitious because it is all so casual because I have been supine. I have tried to say (he thought) I can get along without lovers with only poetry holding the image but the image itself is more important, poetry must grow out of it.

Gabriel came back with his glass full of water which he placed on the table with a crack. He had been and at that moment was contemptuous but was it so nice being wasn't it barren. Maybe I am not an artist he said but I have a stinking hunch artists are made of puppydog tails too. Look at Balzac. Gabriel knew he was talking as though there were even the least valid concept of art in life.

Julian was wondering whether he could be Helen of Troy or Cleopatra better or Juliet with a hand-picked Romeo.

Gabriel raised his eyebrows and became abstract.

Julian's first notice of him was his being seated by a table and talking confidentially to another man. He wore a cap and had black eyes. Julian saw something then that he could want badly, differently from the other tepid wants which he had already that night and morning pushed away. Something now leaped in him, forming his heart into a question mark. He looked at him without moving his eyes away.

Gabriel was brought back to Julian and became restless and said let's get out.

Listen Julian said there's someone back there I want. A worm gnawed his vitals with his heart on top of them like an imbecile's head saying 'How, how is it to be done?'

Gabriel echoed what are you going to do?

Wait! Julian said.

The man's companion left him reading a newspaper. Julian could see the cap on his head. Sometimes he saw the eyes and soon knew that he knew.

All right Julian said. He picked up his own and Gabriel's check and walked to the cashier where he turned and saw who was looking at him and so he was. He turned up the collar on his overcoat and got between the revolving doors.

Gabriel came out too. It was dawn again for him.

'Again' thought Julian is more tragic than remorse.

They walked against the wind. It was 14th Street which only the good escape.

At Union Square Julian said wait and turned his back to the wind. We'll stand here a minute.

The gray was penetrating and would have been even if it did not signify the coming of something. Those who moved by and across were like people with their mouths closed forever. Policemen and newspaper vendors, workers released from their night jobs and other workers, were starting without stopping. The gray was a coating as they waited on the corner. It fell and emanated; it settled. Taxis went slowly or waited and there was a bright peacock blue and silver one which looked like an ecstasy. He didn't stare at it, his eyes were walking along the block they had iust traversed. Gabriel's hair was swaying.

Someone swung out of the cafeteria door. Whoever it was wore a cap and was without an overcoat. He stood a moment before coming; then he too walked against the wind. He was without an overcoat and his trousers wrinkled.

If the wind destroys him Julian thought I shall keep him inside of me. I shall be compelled to keep him continually with me if the wind destroys him. Before anything happens, I shall feel with a permanent hard desire the want of him.

Even when he was exactly opposite Julian he didn't stop and Julian turned so as to look at his back. He saw him wait for a truck to pass and put his hands in his pockets, raising his coat behind. The coat fit him tightly everywhere. Julian saw now for the first time the back of the neck above the back, higher above the buttocks, more so above the calves.

As Julian stood with Gabriel saying not a word he saw him take his feet up and put them down again across Union Square. It was no intention of Julian's to sink through the sidewalk. He saw him almost in the center of Union Square. The blue and silver taxi sounded three yards away. It was unmistakably there; Julian turned his head to see it plainly and touched Gabriel's elbow and went to it.

Gabriel followed and they got in, Julian sitting on the side next to the walk. Its nose was already pointing in the right direction.

Drive across the Square Julian said. They started flying. Slower he said.

The photograph of him came closer and would have passed through half of their bodies if Julian, whose hand had been all the time on the handle of the door of the taxi, had not said to the driver stop. It was in the middle of the Square where they stopped and directly by him with the door of the taxi opening into his face as he turned and no one was there for him to see but Julian. It was so because there was nothing to it but for him to get in the taxi and that is what he did.

Recognition on the sidewalk and recognition in a taxi are two different things. If it was not exceptionally charming that he should remember Julian from some affair it was to Julian since it made him forget grayness and almost his address. Since it made him forget the demons of annoyance and doubt.

Tell him what address Gabriel Julian said. I'll tell him: 319 West Third he said to the driver.

They rode along fast, Julian being informed that his captive worked at night and always ate breakfast at that hour and he was on his way home to bed. He had been born on an island in the Mediterranean.

My eyelids Julian thought are what are tingling most but he wouldn't have sworn to it for his whole body was. They stopped in front of what looked to him like the last place in the world anyone would take anybody and Julian paid the driver forty cents. He used his key and the three of them went in to find Louis and Karel wide awake though lying down, Louis wearing nothing, Karel having on pajamas of no recognizable color.

If he was displeased or surprised he didn't show it. He still wore his cap.

On the balcony where they went Julian found out about his hair because he took his cap off but not his clothes. He had short black hair and it wasn't very soft. He could not be persuaded to go to bed because he wanted Julian to come to his apartment on 16th Street which he shared with two others but they went to work at eight o'clock.

Julian heard Gabriel, Louis and Karel. He could hear the sound of their voices but not

their words. He kissed Danny who had very
white teeth and arms that closed around him.
Danny wouldn't undress and he didn't want to
have that done either but Julian was illicit and
their lips were together so. When it happened
Julian's ears grew into wings.

They came down from the balcony, Julian
having promised to see him at 16th Street two
days from then in the afternoon. Gabriel was
missing. Karel and Louis were yet awake and
looking wan. Julian let Danny out without
kissing him again and locked the door. Giving
Karel and Louis cigarettes he sat on the side of
their bed to rhapsodize. The sun was streaming
in the windows.

Louis said yes Gabriel has just told us you
picked the kind that makes homosexuality worth-
while.

Julian closed his eyes and leaned on his elbow.

Karel said to Louis tell him what else Gabriel
said.

Louis didn't say anything.

Karel said he wanted Louis to take a check
which he saw in your wallet.

Julian sat up. It's a refund from Macy's for
fifty cents!

And not only that, he suggested that Louis go
through the pockets of your friend since this is
Sunday and assuming he was paid Saturday night
and assuming you were going to bed together.

CHAPTER TWELVE : SOMEONE, CUT THEIR TONGUES OUT

KAREL said to Louis, after Julian had left with Frederick for the drag, you know I've been trying to keep you. They were in bed, still above death and wedged into life.

The eyes of Louis went somewhere else but directly to the point. What does that mean he asked that you're getting tired of me?

Were you ever anything about me that could make you grow tired?

Don't use that kind of language. Say what you mean.

Perhaps I choose to be subtle.

Don't be a bitch. What are you looking for? Something like Julian? You homos don't like each other.

Don't be so crude. Just because—

You've got your eyes fixed on the male symbol. Your feet get mixed up with each other's in the rush. You couldn't fall in love with each other.

That's not what I was thinking about. You have a talent for diverting the issue. I've paid homage to that. But I meant something else.

I know what you meant: you think I'm not

6

thinking about *your* symbol. What gave you the idea that I was queer?

Oh—so you're not. I suspected that.

Louis smiled broadly and reached out.

Karel didn't take the embrace but said don't.

You know you like me to do it. Don't you?

Karel shrugged. Of course. Under the proper circumstances.

You guys aren't realists.

You guys are sophists.

Say, Karel, don't talk to me like that. You're talking like a kid.

You're eating an apple said Karel.

Are you trying to be funny?

Karel stared at him. I admit that you've given me... Tears came to his eyes.

Dont cry my dear Louis said. Didn't you want me to put my arm around you?

Wait Karel said.

So you don't love me any more. Well, whom have you fallen in love with?

Nobody yet.

Nobody? I should think someone around here...

So you're reconciled to the fact that I don't love you?

Louis looked at him and said listen Karel your love doesn't matter a damn. You're deceiving yourself about this business of love. If you ever imagined that you were in love with me, you were mistaken. In fact, you couldn't fall in love with anybody. You're interested in approximating something.

Approximating what?

Being a—say, why do I have to be explaining things to you? You don't like explanations.

I hate to think that I have to require them. Whatever value you give certain things, Louis, doesn't affect their existence.

What do you mean doesn't affect their existence?

I mean that you're destroying an illusion.

Louis was serious. Destroying an illusion? Yes, I am. But you ought to be above that. You're not like these other homos—you're intelligent.

That makes no difference.

Makes no difference? Well, then, why are you interested in explanations? Like all wenches, I suppose, you dont really believe in your intuitions. I realize you're imperfect.

On the contrary, I think you're quite perfect, Louis, only now you don't coincide.

Let's go to sleep!

Go to sleep. The insult was in him.

Sure, I mean GO TO SLEEP my dear.

I'm not going to sleep yet.

Not yet eh? What do you want me to do for you. Have a cigarette. Karel lit one for him. Come here Louis said.

I'm serious said Karel.

No doubt you are serious Karel.

What made you tell Gabriel and those girls that I was whoring for you?

So Julian told you that did he? Are you always so impressed with what Julian says?

Why did you say it?

I know I was wrong, but you know how it is, I wanted to make an impression on the women. But what difference does it make?

It was simply cheap and I shouldn't stand for it.

But you're not really going to let it make any difference in your attitude are you? You ought to know those cunts—

Listen, Louis. You know it's not the simple fact they think a lie about me—it's the fact that you'd tell them such a thing.

I should have remembered you're sentimental. And I shouldn't have said it.

It isn't only that.

No?

You put me in an evil position. I'm not asking for anything complicated from you.

I know you're not!

Wait! You know everything I've given I've given naturally, because it was the thing to do, but I expected natural behavior in return. For a while...

For a while you thought you were getting it— that's a characteristic conclusion.

So you mean that your behavior hasn't been natural?

No—I mean that it's natural for you to con-clude that natural behavior is agreeable.

I'm not precisely in the mood for subtleties of that sort Louis.

Louis laughed.

I suppose that means you think I'm naive Karel said.

Don't be so positive about your limitations Karel. You're not naive. I can't fool you. Is your confidence waning?

There was a knock. Karel got up to go and it was Gabriel.

Oh—Gabriel Louis said.

It was Gabriel indeed thought Karel, Gabriel with a look down to the ground and then up again in a way that was no apostrophe to the world.

Who has a cigarette? Gabriel asked.

Napoleon's voice at Waterloo thought Karel yet Napoleon was a hero. Without heeding Gabriel's question he slipped over Louis into his place in bed, drawing the covers comfortably up.

Here are some Louis said reaching to the floor and handing the pack to him.

You haven't got a match have you? Karel's furtive eyes saw the bland hysterical corners of Gabriel's mouth. He could hear Gabriel walk to the couch and sit down.

Louis twisted around. Take your things off Gabriel. You haven't been to sleep so why not stay here.

Gabriel's eyes fell daintily upon the cigarette whose ashes he was depositing. His mouth assumed daintiness. No I haven't slept he said.

Get in bed then Louis said resuming his position.

Gabriel arose suddenly.

Karel was on his elbow. Gabriel he said you had better sleep on the couch.

On the couch! said Gabriel. I don't want to sleep on the couch. He had put his hand up to untie his cravat.

Oh you can sleep in here said Louis. There's enough room for him Karel, move over.

Karel looked at Gabriel's morose dislocated face. No he said. It's impossible. The couch is very comfortable. There's nothing wrong with it. I can't sleep with three in a bed.

Sure you can. Come on Gabriel said Louis jerking his head toward the bed.

Karel sat up. Louis I said no.

Come on Karel I'm going to sleep Gabriel said walking directly to them.

You'll have to sleep on the couch Gabriel said Karel.

Say are you going to argue about a bed? The eyes and the mouth were performing Gabriel.

Jesus Karel Louis said the guy's sleepy!

He can sleep on the couch Karel said and lay back.

Listen Karel said Gabriel pressing his knees against the side of the bed. I don't like your goddamn respect for beds. When they have the importance you give them they cease to be a utility and become a fairy's luxury.

You've emphasised their point for the last ten minutes Gabriel Karel said.

I've emphasised nothing Gabriel was raising his voice. I've stood for your petty values as long as I intend to, see? Im going to get out and I'm not coming back!

Don't get yourself excited Gabriel Louis said.

Karel was sitting up. His face was as pale as Gabriel's.

I've got a place to sleep tonight. I didn't come to you guys for a bed said Gabriel his glance sweeping up to the balcony. I didn't pay you the compliment of asking for a place to sleep.

Listen Gabriel said Karel. You don't impress me with these histrionics.

Histrionics? cried Gabriel. You and your values stink! I've been on to you all along. I'm leaving here, see. I'm not going to have anything to do with you. I'm not even going to know you on the streets when I see you. But don't get in my way—

Is that so? said Karel. I know what's eating you Gabriel. You're beaten. You know who's managed this situation ever since it began and you can't stand it any longer.

Don't talk to me Gabriel said slowly his mouth stretching into a whip. You can't talk to me. I've permitted you to talk to me in the past because you fitted into a certain scheme. But beds aren't in my scheme. Say, you might as well give up poetry. What you have to say you can say in bed. You've said it in bed all along. Verse has been just a formality.

I can pass over that Gabriel said Karel. What's the matter with you is that you're a Napoleon without an army. You can't find one here, that's all.

Listen to what I'm saying Karel said Gabriel. You stink! You stink so badly that I don't want to smell you any more. I don't like the smell of your bed. It's all right as long as you don't implicate me in it. But the minute you bring your smell out on the street I'll have it disposed of. And before I go I want to wish you a forest of pricks with an *ocean of glue* because you'll never be able to hold them any other way!

Gabriel wheeled and went and the door came back because he made it.

———

CHAPTER THIRTEEN : I DON'T WANT TO BE A DOLL

IT was a long ride on the subway to 155th Street but they hadn't the money for a taxi. Frederick was not in drag nor was Julian who wore striped pants with a coat that didn't match, his black shirt with an orange tie and a slouch cap. Frederick was not made up more than usual except his eyebrows were plucked thinner but Julian had on his face the darkest powder he could borrow, blue eyeshadow and several applications of black mascara; on his lips was orange-red rouge and a brown pencil had been on his eyebrows showing them longer. He wanted to be considered in costume and so get in for a dollar less. When they arrived at the Casino Palace policemen and others were about the entrance. They passed under the canopy and went in.

I hope we don't get arrested tonight Julian said. Your judgement of my trousers is true but your moral wrong he thought, getting his ticket cheaper than Frederick who said I wonder if money will ever be as unimportant as I think it is.

They had to wind up a long gold-banistered

staircase above which a terrible racket was taking serene form.

There is only one sex—the female said Frederick.

Now they are doing without beauty said Julian when he saw the first creation. It was all black lace but only stockings and step-ins and brassiere and gloves. Fanny Ward is supposed to come.

Yes my dear Frederick said. She's so young she has to learn to play the piano all over again!

The ball was too large to be rushed at without being swallowed. The negro orchestra on the stage at one end was heard at the other end with the aid of a reproducer. On both sides of the wall a balcony spread laden with people in boxes at tables. Underneath were more tables and more people. The dancefloor was a scene whose celestial flavor and cerulean coloring no angelic painter or nectarish poet has ever conceived.

This place is neither cozy nor safe Frederick said. It's lit up like high mass.

One was with blonde hair and a brown face and yellow feathers and another was with black hair and a tan face and white feathers. Some had on tango things and some blue feathers. One wore pink organdie and a black picture hat. There were many colors including a beard in a red ballet skirt and number 9 shoes and some others who, conjuring with their golden-tipped wands against the voices of their mutually male con-

sciences, yet remained more serious than powdered
—they seemed to be always on their way to far off
mistresses.

They found Tony and Vincent at a table with
K-Y and Woodward. Vincent spoke with the
most wonderful whisky voice Frederick! Julian!
Tony was South American. He had on a black
satin that Vincent had made him, fitted to the
knee and then flaring, long pearls and pearl drops.

Tony dear aren't you overdressed! asked Frederick.

I suppose *you* would say overdressed Tony
answered but I'm not Sheba surrounded by food
and Mary what you look like in that outfit he said
to Julian. Look at her!

Vincent had on a white satin blouse and black
breeches. Dear I'm master of ceremonies tonight
and you should have come in drag you'd have
gotten a prize. He had large eyes with a sex-life
all their own and claimed to be the hardest boiled
queen on Broadway. Frederick he said you look
like something Lindbergh dropped on the way
across. Dry yourself Bella!

When are you going to remove your mask and
reveal a row of chamber pots Frederick replied
in his resonant voice which could also be nasal
at the wrong time.

The music was playing wavy and sad and so true.

Let's dance Julian said to K-Y and they went
on the floor.

You've mastered the art of makeup she said.

I must have he said when I did things that were pleasant surprises, not wicked because they were unusual and necessary.

Dancing drew the blood faster through their bodies. Drink drusic drowned them. A lush annamaywong lavender-skinned negro gazed at him.

They are looking this way so hard said Julian their eyes go through us and *button* in the back.

A boy with an innocent exterior said to him over his shoulder how is your dog bite?

My dog bite Julian said sweetly. Your mouth hasn't been that close to my leg all evening.

This is dreadully amusing said K-Y.

One may divide people into thrills and frills I think Julian said. What he was really thinking was that it must be the white-pink flesh like some Italians with the lippink scarlet as heliotrope and the black of hair and the eyebrows with the miraculous slant bespeaking benevolence. He knew the precise youth of it there and the vulgarity raw enough to be exhilarating. He saw another as they danced by a table and the sharkmouth of a hope tore his womb, carrying a piece of it away.

Someone shouted Bessie if you don't believe Heliogabalus died by having his head stuck in a toilet bowl you NEEDN'T COME AROUND any more.

They all ought to be in a scrap-book Julian said. Would blood, paste and print make them stick together?

No said K-Y. There is no holding people back. It will go on until it stops and then there will be something else.

shut your hole watching
them for a moment but when she opened her upstairs cunt and started to belch the greetings of the season I retired in a flurry her boyfriend with the imperfect lacework in the front of his mouth
was a thunderclap could indeed would have been gentler Fairydale Bedagrace a prize bull in the 2000 pound class and his proud owner is Harry A.
Koch there's my Uncle looking for
me Beulah calm your bowels two o'clock and not a towel wet that
would be both justice and
amusement Jim! I told you to stay home and mind the babies wished for nothing better well who could? than a man lover and a woman lover in the same
bed ladies and gentlemen I was born in Sydney Australia twenty-two years
ago everything nowadays to invent something right things have been wrong so
long has wanted to break away but couldn't find me anywhere else so he changed his
mind come on Margie come on Helen the

usher on the right side said to sit on the left side
the usher on the left side said to sit on the right
side so we'll sit in the *mid*dle Who pushed
   me aw look what your old man got for
   pushing I may be wrong but I think he's
   wonderful kiss it you bastard listen
   Kate whoops Mr. Cunningham! there's
Mr. Cunningham I said feel it not play with it thank
   YOU wouldn't that jar your mother's
   preserves the
   French are so easy to enrage poor dears close
the coffin lid the
   STEnch dont think about it analysis will kill
   it I'm ever so much obliged shit
   mother my feet
   stink the pantry is full and the toilet articles
burst with expectation all that's needed is
   love aren't you the one I'd
   hate to go beyond it unless taken by a
   guide
   what would I find a fatuous madness that I've
found
   get a load of her a skin like the bark of a
   canteloupe he's a
   quEry goody goody
   goody for our side we've won the chocolate
   cake madam I haven't said a word I haven't
   spOken dearie it wouldn't take much coaching
to make you lisp into the
   grave did you see that

basket your opinions don't change your **appear-**
ance I thought they wOuld she
peddles her can
with her one avoids far worse
things I'd rather be Spanish than
mannish he eats
it some things aRe like a fall down
stairs so few people know anything at all about
the general subject of
grace beautiful can come out of him because
he's just clean
clay I came home Flora and found her in one
bed drunk with her eyes made up
and I want to have the texture of
it look you Up and dowN one
meets no end of celebrities all having nothing
to do with
sex it's a false landscape only art giving it full
colors
picked me up on Eighth Street and did me for
trade in Christopher Street some
books aren't even read things
about the Village because they are bound to be
ninety percent
lies there a new place called Belle's Jeans it
must be horribly vulgar if
I had your money
baby think that liking is
knowing of Laura with wistfulness the hard
poor girl no Miss Suckoffski smelt the

worst Miss Johnnie didn't smell she just lay
there I closed her door after two pages had
slipped in my esophagus I've been getting up with
a cold ever since all they omitted was the
diaper laid out every last corpse though it took
us till
dawn the kind of wit servants could be tipped
with if they could use it had
trembled so he said my but you're
sensitive that old auntie please! once
confessed his love for a man so I didn't stand
up and wave the flag I just sat there you know me
Mabel and
smiled Mr. Schubert get OFF my face I can't
see the CONtract the wine came up and he looked
at my intellect so often got
out of the way of a big truck and put my hand
over my cunt like
this just too bad isn't it buttercup scalps
of her victims of which she must have cabinets
full says he wears a flower in his buttonhole
because it simply Wont stay in his
hair! memories are
best couldn't stomach his crotch once so he
would be spiteful a kiss is a
promise she looks like death's daughter brought
in backwards and went
up bold as you please dropped my lilac
robe could hardly get two articulate sentences
out on the subject of homosexuality before

someone interrupted us Phoebe-Phobia in person
not a college pennant she had one in her hand
though that bore a distinct
   resemblance ninety-five percent of the world
is just naturally queer and are really according to
the degree of
   resistance I don't say I *do* and I don't say I *don't*
but if the fur coat had fit me he would have had a
DIFferent answer people
   do better than you think they
   do in these days men will be great if they have
to walk out as
   skeletons living I learned from the inside with
a big old Queen Kitty I laid her to
   filth likes to abhor people and it's all liking
the end I
   suppose strangely mature like the
   continent very
   sensual and sees a reason for discipling apparently because she can't live without
   comfort suddenly as suddenly always
   is lit up like a country
   church empty couch took it out of me rather
didn't take it out of
   me divine not at all only human ever
   saying life words can
   always afford to be tolerant of that which we
   misunderstand likes the brave dear that one
best
   some Lesbians make me think of alligators I

saw a little girl holding up one in the movies and
the angles seemed so
    characteristic fancy work done at
    home and if I look real a definition of love isn't
    needed seven yards of lace
    curtain six of the finest rats jumped
    out spoke to me said it was a good racket I
should keep it up I was good at it he held my arm
my dear as we walked back after I had petrified
four or five males who walked into the tea-room
two standing before the urinal dying to and yet
so embarrassed waiting for my permission to
pull their things out and another said standing still
on entering my leg being strung across the wash
    basin blind as a bat screaming for the
    daylight excuse me for putting this bromide
in pink curlpapers take them off in the
    morning did not shit Miss Bitch though she's
here according to farts deprived
    of house and home if
    one does needlework one has to talk too such
genteel innocent malice is almost more than
human flesh can bear I mean the tongue gets
mixed up with the needle your mouth is
    bleeding Belle! but the clock doesn't stop when
somebody is
    hit seems to have adopted the habits of a
gentleman in every particular which naturally
includes the payment of paramours if only in
bohemian

dinners Becky could you spare it?
the macabre is not omitted from any universe
why not find it in his
bread-box she's a flag that's never been taken
down I'm sure he draws lewd pictures in spare
moments and tears them up in tears and speaking
of tears could you ever be drowned in
them makes me think of a Christmas tree been
standing all
year has a fish
hooves? looks at one through oceans of lemonade
slightly sweet slightly
sour empty as paper
bags can't you tell by his manner that he lives
on an
hallucination she's a whole egg upheld by the
shimmering sea of
humanity what's the use of knowing people if
not to attack their souls or what they consider
inviolable? the universal stillbirth or homicide
in the womb you
were made to walk along with me and speak
to me like
that the first thing I knew she was groping me
like
mad thinks she has the only bedroom back at
the
ball does he rent his brains my
dear just dirt you
silly! loose as a cut

jockstrap
still dead as far as my mouth
goes a
big chisler while he was here feature it
adores me to stick it in his and flew into a
temper last night when after the regular party my
poor thing wouldn't get a hard on enough to go in
and STAY in but I promised to do my husbandly
duty next
time orgasm right in his
pants it may have been the first intimate intro-
duction to Miss 69 in
person is to be a comfort standing in a tall
scooped out penislike
niche squiffy on
weed observe my dear the bloated lemons
waiting to be
selected the first Bess ever to conceive a hopeless
romantic affection for
me thrill market the
haughty after breakfast hour grime
in the creases parting his hair has given him a
new better
flavor discovered a brazen speakeasy with
awfully good stuff
cheap mentioned something about a hashish
party please
noticing my excellent features and asking why
I didn't have a screen test taken until a professional
routine came into his

compliments flew down on special
wheels couldn't say no to the sensations he gives
me gayest thing on two
feet harlot making theatrical costumes like one
demented and renting the
bed them to come down here and fight like
mEn startling
expert symmetry she wanted to make
her have a cuter sissylip
one never say anus you mUst have been stunned
into
chillness said why and I said I wanted to see
whether he would 69 and he said of course he
didn't and I said but he
did may look Chinese but she's American can
you imagine he wanted to brown I mean bugger
me woman quite mad so cunty in her dark land
so idiosyncratic and blind so obvious so abnormal
only
fairy voice about 20 made me really
pretty oh you twisted piece of
lilac the curtain's going
up
looks like the wrath of
God aroma one of Harvard and autumn leaves
the Russian ballet hanging on the wall of his
heart dished as though
drunken showing
everything mattress on the
floor Byzantine

baggage grand cocksucker
fascinated by fairies of the Better
Class chronic
liar fairy
herself sexual
estimate crooning I'M A CAMPfire girl
gratuitous sexually meaning
both my thighs are so much
stouter tongue's hanging
out sprawled in
bed lower than my
navel tie beginning between his
breasts nest of
Lesbians eyebrows so perfect what it is to
blossom before his style started going uphill
on one-ballbearing rollerskates and the curious
pain
began Norma Shearer hairbob the wild evening
one and they turned the spot on me with applause
hisses pennies tenderness in sex you know I hate
nothing God has bursting breakfast for two Daisy
he's the type that's aged by its prospects taken
for 18 tonight by a broker make this another leaf
in your hair my dear stunning seaman dreadful
bugger sort of jaw coming from the sort of neck
with an open collar that flattens wombs huge
meat that's why no matter how many publishers'
offices she unpacked her undies in she couldn't
give old man Criticism a hard on sped on his
way cradle days! crushed her like I always do asks

to be insulted and you know my rule Anna
said have you seen Pauline's novel I said intimat-
ing that it's good? said it's an act of God! said
I have no doubt there are so many objects for
criticism they Must come from a source so
abundant never cease shocking with his diseases
hide it in your vagina and carry on do you have
to go into a song and dance about a face artist
turn over kid I want to use you

At the table again they had gin and Frederick
asked who'd want sillymadness for a sister and
Woodward said I would if I had to have a sister.
Woodward was sitting, knowing that K-Y was
cheating and loving, a real gun girl of the soul.
He had never gone to the bottom of her in the
real heavenly way. She thought she was a sea
and he didn't.

You look like bread with the butter on backwards Vincent was saying to Frederick.

You Frederick answered look as though you
had just been ejected from God's private office
having gone there on ILLEGITIMATE BU-
SINESS.

Don't say anything more Vincent cried would
you tear my soul from my body?

Someone spoke to Woodward and passed on.

Who is that? asked Julian.

He looks like a bunch of uninteresting nerves
said Frederick.

Anyway he's a dope peddler Woodward said.

He looked almost frightened said Julian.

Probably at your youth K-Y said.

Music for the grand march started and Vincent leapt away and the procession began. He threw his fingers everyway and went with the music from one to another and they stepped by slowly with their hands on their hips or one hand on one hip or an arm up or both arms and wreathed in smiles and all made up within an inch of their lives. There were screams to them and hand-clappings and they waved from their high heels. Fifty or more walked one by one to the platform with a spotlight on it and steps on two sides and there Vincent was. They mounted and turned with Vincent showing them off for the prizes given for the most applause, supposedly, for the most beautiful costumes, but he gave them to those he knew no matter how much they pushed and tore. There were half a dozen running around crying I GOT FIRST PRIZE and others got other prizes and the music went on.

Julian swayed through the tables and was grabbed by the hand and pulled to one table for a drink of rye and told his eyes were beautiful. He stayed there until someone came from another table and got him and gave him a drink of gin and said kiss me but he said you don't look expectant. That one followed him toward the orchestra and he went in the side door and up on the stage and kissed the leader and asked him to play something. When he went back down the steps the door was closed into the hall and the one who had given him the drink of gin was standing in front of it. Julian knew that people had to forget appearances, that horses would hardly, that mountains and clouds wouldn't and neither would some men but this one would. He found he could be mad and wasn't afraid of the vengeance of God nor its earthly equivalent and there was no hesitation from beginning to end. He came out fanning himself. A chaplet to go around my neck he thought.

Vincent rushed to him and shouted have you got a cent on you Phil wait for me after it's over and we'll go to Child's Paramount or pick up a couple of broads and take them up to the joint and *camp like mad*!

Julian confided in him what had just happened. Yes? Cut me in TWO and sew me up with needle and thread! Vincent said. Was he large?

Julian said I'll see you in the poolroom and went to the laboratory to piss and become a little sick. Since he thought he would get that way he stood in front of the urinal for a long, long time.

When he felt better he went out with a hundred images clawing at him, some good, some almost good and some almost painful.

This is how dolorous things can be in high fettle. The hall was the garden of Eden afterwards and the lights were out. There was a queen's sorrow in it too. He walked to a gleam coming from under a door and tried the knob but it wouldn't work. He banged on it until someone came and unlocked it from the outside.

He was being looked in the face by several policemen one of whom immediately said THAT'S THE ONE.

What one? Julian asked innocently.

No it's not said another and the first one agreed and Julian walked away. He was around the corner and doubted if he would take the right subway. Vincent was not to be seen nor anyone he knew. A short man in neat clothes said hello to him.

Julian said hello.

How are you? the man said.

I'm all right said Julian.

Where are you going?

I'm going home.

Let's go have a cup of coffee.

Julian said all right and they went into a coffee pot in the next block. Julian had two eggs also and the man who was a soft comfortable personality who glurred at the right moments paid for them.

They were out on the street when the man said do you live around here?

Julian told him that he lived downtown.

What's your address?

Julian told it to him.

I'll come to see you sometime.

All right said Julian.

The man showed him the elevated and Julian thanked him.

He went up the steps and there were no velvet carpets, no flutes, no bells, no incense and no dancing girls.

In the car he was alone except for a man who looked like a football player never recovered from a daze he got once while scrimmaging.

I'm glad I have my beauty he thought if ever so little weary. Am I a doll he thought or some kind of ghost believing in everything I have believed in do I know what marriage is what new texture is in it anything more than a tongue and lips and inexpert teeth oh to be a bright and unschooled lass I know it and love it and know it and leave it and know it and hate it but never too much the stalk up the poor lavender buds clinging to it their mouths closed yellow in the green and dug clean for anything I've found in the oystergray marrow to hell with all junior disorders what are they my next lover must teach me to swear love is a thing to know more of and deeper of or nothing is lost ? nothing can be helped is better life is made up of crossing sticks and time.

The crying in him was because everything was all wrong and he knew it as all learn it sometimes: wrong yet magnetic, prolonged yet brief.

At Sixth Avenue and Eighth Street he got out. It was scarcely dawn.

A doll does not believe in itself he thought it believes only in its dollness I have the will to doll which is a special way of willing to live my poetry may merely be a way of dolling up and then it may be the beginning of ego I think I would be practically nothing without my poetry unless a DOLL my homosexuality is just a habit to which I'm somehow bound which is little more than a habit in that it's not love or romance but a dim hard fetich I worship in my waking dreams it's more a symbol of power than a symbol of pleasure not a symbol inducing pleasure but exemplifying it not a specific symbol no I am not a fairy doll.

On Third Street he used his key for the door. There was Karel in bed with one hand behind his neck. He seemed to be sleeping with his eyes open.

Where is Louis? Julian asked though not caring particularly to know.

Love? said Karel without changing his eyes and speaking softly. Horror! Has that word escaped my lips again? O divine power. O hymn of praise. I am too weak to hear it. I cannot lift my voice.

Do you love him desperately? asked Julian.

If I could only go over America painlessly from now on said Karel give me the needle doctor. Imagine the state of the poor girl sent to the hospital continually I mean America by Mr. Wriggle. She lived next door to him in Baltimore and spread her big brown bossy buttocks for him on the Montana plains but in New York she's homeless and the Round Table isn't exactly the place is it? She came in carpet slippers hanging on to Mr. Wriggle's arm like she wanted to be back home or at least on the prairie where there was room and I'm telling you when Mr. Wriggle brought his thing out and tried to put it in her it was time for somebody to laugh. And so Harold laughed you should have seen the poor thing's eyes roll feeling Mr. Wriggle's thing inside her and moving around the edges. I didn't know whether to laugh or sob or To Help but I felt like saying stop Eli she'll only carry the memory of you to her grave to bury it because it's a shame to her. Karel was wiping the tears away.

What's the matter with you? Julian said.

She never lies down or even sits Karel laughed through his tears she's older than the headless horseman and even more eternal.

O dove's puff! Julian said beginning to undress.

I sometimes think of poor little Miss Rector Karel continued who tried so much to crawl away from her skin but succeeded only in coming out with a hard on and then skidding right back again. Do you know I don't think I ever told you Julian two days later he called me over the phone and said that he had to have five dollars so next morning I met him. I met him on the street having just cashed a check from the *Sun*. I took it out and handed it to him and wanted to know how he felt about homosexuality and he told me.

You must have paid for the information Julian said.

How far away and insignificant it is and yet not insignificant.

Julian was removing his makeup over the sink. I suppose you used to paint his arm muscles lilac with your tongue he said.

Lilac or blackberrywaste I don't remember which Karel said.

I think he must have been influenced by Louis said Julian. Did he fancy himself as your intellectual mentor and physical disciple?

Yes Karel said but he was detestable later developing a manner socially and artistically repellent to the last degree. Megalomania with particularly bad blood into the bargain. Oh God, how can I live another life? Will it begin all over again? Oh God, this vessel is frail.

Julian emerged in his pajamas. Are you going to sleep anymore or haven't you slept?

Karel didn't move. What could be bitterer than love or stink worse on a cold day he asked.

Mrs. Dodge of course said Julian. Let me get in with you. He got in.

Karel's speech came to life and he said what is one to do on this planet tied to George Bernard Shaw, Gandhi and other weekend guests.

Gandhi in this century's answer to Christ Julian said.

Karel covered his eyes with a hand. Have you seen John Wannamaker's windows dear? Not even father Alive and Breathing by the fireside could be more elegiac. The only horror left would be resurrection.

Brains will fall out especially from corpses Julian said. He wasn't sleepy but he felt so bad he had to dredge the spontaneous. Have you any ideas about happiness Karel?

Not really said Karel. Even when ideas about happiness amount to common morality they are no less important than mine but I'm talking morality anyway and morality is rotten.

Why?

Because it's a stage of rot. It's the skin beginning to fall off.

Yes but about happiness can't we argue ourselves somehow into it?

Happiness is Being not Knowing and let it go but I say Knowing is not quite but almost happiness. Being can go where it pleases said Karel.

Let it go Julian said. One begins to have

ideas about happiness as soon as one sees that happiness is impossible.

If I went down entirely I could be happy, knowing nothing, but his mouth drew away and I'm still here Karel said. Here, Mr. Policeman, here do what you will with me.

And speaking of deceptive appearances I think of all the live people wearing death so impassively Julian said.

My YES would have to be beaten up with the white of an egg and set to chill on his body. Karel laughed as though he were still weeping.

The point is Julian said sleepily that the amount of stupidity is never equaled by the amount of elimination by the individual intellect.

Karel said some of them not only wear death they wear it out and then lie in coffins as though it were new, in fact all dead people look as though life were still fresh in their minds but that's as far as it all goes: they can't wholly disappear.

It's the handsome ones I pity most said Julian.

Pity is love after a while. My chest hurts said Karel.

You mean love becomes pitylove and finally pity. Love of all kinds does. I love you.

You don't know what love is said Karel turning his cheek over. You've never wanted me so that every line of me made you ache.

What does my love mean then?

It may be some minor pathology. Whether it is or not I love it.

You love my love for you.

Yes. It is a little curious and a little strange. Believe that I am perfectly truthful now.

But isn't love want?

But what want? What form is this want? Is it affection or something mystic? Where is the line between the strange and the common?

Perhaps love is loneliness Julian said. Simple, honest loneliness.

But that would be common.

My love isn't wholly common.

Julian you know how little I feel for people, how little anyone has now to give me even of naïveté or resistance. I mean pure pleasure except in physical beauty is almost out of the question. I like seeing Louis and Gabriel act but there is nothing between them and me now: nothing but disgusting trivial acts.

What do you mean?

I'll tell you. You're very selfish is what I've noticed about you; unwilling that is to forget yourself and certain definite preconceived ideas or plans. Maybe I am one of these plans.

And you don't love me.

I do love you but only because you do not disturb me, you face the way I do and you are moving in that direction, and so turn to me with sweet words in your throat that are altogether

for me, addressed to no one else.   Maybe that is
the way you feel about me.

But such an explanation is too cold.

Perhaps it is because it is all necessary, perhaps
that is why it is at all.

It is too sterile said Julian.

That is always the artist's plaint Karel said.
I feel around me a great coarse essentially foreign
world in which only the *objets d'art* seem friendly,
seem able to walk and talk with me.

When you think of the number of superfluous
but exact people.

Let me go on, life.   How many understand
cadence Karel said.

Do you?

One can't do anything about medieval statues
can one the same of Eliot.   That sentence is a
study in cadence.

You are always untrue if you go far enough
said Julian.

The experience of space Karel went on is the
elimination of dirt and that is outer.   The experience of time is the growth of everything in the
body to the very pores and that is inner.

I suppose the end comes said Julian when the
pores can't blow out any more.

Both are divine Karel said accident and inevitability.

No! said Julian.

Accident is that for which we are insufficiently

prepared and inevitability is that for which we are even more insufficiently prepared. Louis has left me.

Birds of plumage screamed through the room.

What do you mean, he's left you Julian said getting more and more sleepy.

I mean he's gone.

He'll come back murmured Julian. He'll come back like a door closing on your littlest finger.

No he won't come back said Karel. He's with Gabriel for good this time and when he left he took your typewriter and a suitcase of my manuscripts. I yelled for the police but none came and then I cried.

There was a lovely dead silence with a white, white face who opened its lips and said what difference does it make what difference does it make to me and then went to sleep.

CHAPTER FOURTEEN: CRUISE

THERE is something in my mind Frederick said.
Is it big? asked Julian.
It must be Broadway Karel said.
Or! Frederick's lips were prominent.
Shut up said Karel.
Broadway is big with bright lights said Julian
and a torso passed with a head. It was walking
in the direction opposite the one in which they
were walking.
Are you going back? asked Frederick.
What did I see? asked Julian.
It wasn't fate—
Not in the form of a woman.
Well are you Frederick said.
No said Julian look at it.
It is big Karel said that is why you, too, are
big looking at it. You can't decide can you.
You are not the only one Frederick said
ooooooooOOO.
Don't camp like that Karel said. Or I'll
leave.
You musn't leave said Frederick. I'll go
with—
Go ahead Julian said.

They stopped; people passed when they stopped.

There are such things as eyes Karel thought such things as are not eyes as words as even arms.

Let's go on Frederick said look over there.

Broadway can dance as well as walk Karel thought. Only it is not dancing now although it might just have been dancing.

The taxis came, went, wheeled from beneath their feet.

I feel like screaming whirred Frederick.

Hush said Karel.

Look at those two Frederick said ignoring him and they all tried to look.

Broadway is a big long place like a hall Karel was thinking, with new bodies and old doors that are not important but the bodies are and the clothes. And the faces. Broadway is alive with I don't know what all but I do know with some things, it is alive with people not in bed. It is alive with people not in bed he said aloud his hands cold in his overcoat's pockets.

Oh yes said Frederick.

There it is again Julian said isn't it. He meant the torso.

Yes it is Frederick said.

Karel looked and saw that it was.

Julian had slowed. I'm turning around he said.

Well said Karel.

Alone? asked Frederick.

Why not Julian said and went on.

He's got his own key Karel said.

Frederick said I have some money and would Karel like something to drink. Karel didn't mind and they turned into 46th Street and went up some steps. At the top of the second flight Frederick rang a bell outside a door. They were looked at through an uncovered hole and admitted.

The place was milling with mostly men who looked young. Some of them had curled hair. Clothes that fit were on others.

There was a separate room in which was a victrola and a Spanish boy doing high-kicks and splits. He was surrounded by different ones at tables. Karel and Frederick went to the bar in the other room. Karel thought he saw Vincent and Tony at a table in the room with the Spanish boy but it was so dim there he wasn't sure.

They ordered Old-Fashioned cocktails and looked around and seeing nothing that interested them in their present mood, after the second drink nothing would do for Frederick but that he should suggest they go up on the Drive.

Karel was willing but lingered until they were spoken to by two undesirables. Frederick was frantic about one until he discovered on the other side of his neck a large boil.

Karel said to Frederick I will go up on the Drive for I'm dying for it.

They went out and down and over to the bus

stop and took a bus and sat on the top of it until 106th Street or higher. There they got off and started to walk but first they both had to piss and that was rather pleasing.

They got up on Riverside Drive again. Soon there was a lot of sailors and civilians who must have started to follow them. Karel and Frederick could hear them, at first a crowd of them but neither dared look back.

Let's hurry Karel said. Let's cross. He heard them coming and calling out things. He would not stop nor would Frederick. Automobiles passed and they dashed across.

Karel said ooh and Frederick cried ohoooh. They were on the park space and on the gravel and almost by the buildings.

When Karel did turn around they were leaping at Frederick and him. He saw Frederick get swiped. One swung, one sailor, at Karel who had to run then across to two automobiles parked where some people were. He heard pad pad after him but was Frederick being killed.

Keep away from him the men in the cars said and two backed back. The men in the cars said you shouldn't be out on the Drive at this hour.

Karel turned and saw Frederick lying on the ground a thin figure far away. He saw him get up and move to the sidewalk RUN. He ran forward a little and as he took Frederick by the arm he saw two of them run at him again and he said let's RUN. They ran up one street and Frederick could say hail the first taxi but no taxi could be seen. What they did see was a private car and it stopping and the two chasing them were gaining on them. The audacity, the cussedness Karel thought as one had tried to hit him before that one sailor had his fly open the white showing.

The car was stopping. Two men got out and Frederick cried SAVE US FROM THESE SAILORS! The sailors were there and the men holding them off said to Frederick and Karel get in the car.

You're safe all right they said. They grabbed the sailors and said we're policemen you'll have to come along.

There was a crowd gathering and both sailors were trying to get away.

Karel had his handkerchief out, spitting on it and wiping off the mascara.

One of the sailors broke away and one of the policemen chased him.

The other sailor whined let me go I want to get away and the other policeman, cursing him, took out a blackjack and hit him on the shoulder which somewhat quieted him.

Frederick moaned now we're done for.

The other sailor didn't come back nor did Karel's eyebrows after the way he rubbed them.

The policeman that was left got in the car.

They went to the police station and marched to
the sergeant's desk. The whole gang had followed
and were ordered out. Karel heard the policeman
say fast thissailorsaidhefuckedhiminthemouthbut
theresnocomplaintsoitsdisorderlyconductforall.

Karel's heart did not sink. He had been
through it so many times in his mind he thought
now life is being merely pedantic. He noticed
the electric lights in particular.

What is your name (in a harsh voice)? Leers:
search them! Contents of Frederick's pockets:
two eyebrow tweezers, one black makeup pencil
(with protector), one over-size ring twiddled by the
detective, papers, key, money. The money was
returned and the rest kept. Contents of Karel's
pockets: one black makeup pencil (with protector),
comb, key, money, all returned but makeup pencil
and Karel thought I'll have to buy a new one.

Go in there.

They entered a kind of waiting room. Karel
had a slight headache.

Frederick said you don't seem much perturbed
how can you take it like that? I envy you.

Karel shrugged, thinking the occasion required
no more confirmation than that.

They strolled in and out making wisecracks and
Karel said to them you're all convinced beforehand why say anything.

One said if you'd stayed on Broadway this
wouldna happened.

Karel looked sarcastically and said something about Broadway not that I know it so well.

Frederick told Karel that all the while his voice was sissy.

For Christ's sake Karel said I don't appear cowed anyway. He tried to appear just a little incommoded.

One perfectly unmentionable creature Frederick thought came in and said pair of the girls huh?

Karel looked at him as though he had just said no haven't a light buddy sorry.

Frederick was looking morose.

Karel thought that the sailor was cute looking with a sweet mouth. Anyway he's not so hoity toity by this time the concupiscent bugger.

Well on my life Karel caught himself saying as he was looking at one spot and there suddenly appeared the visage of one Carl Manor, poet, who murmured well what are you doing here?

Karel smiled. He was noticing that Carl Manor had several what you might call abrasions, contusions, swellings and spots on his face and was being dressed by a surgeon. Two tough guys had just beat him up and there they were so Karel thought well ha, ha, that's that, no loss to poetry!

Frederick was watching the clock for the time to come. It did come and with it the patrol wagon. They all marched into it and there were some boys looking at them and they were taken to the station next to Harold's domicile.

After saying their names very plainly to the turnkey Frederick and Karel were given a cell to themselves. There was nothing but one long hard bench and a spigot above a toilet bowl.

Frederick answered yes you can drink from it if you can stand the stench coming from below.

The bench was calculated to be all but unendurable for two people.

Frederick said I can't sleep can you?

I don't know Karel said.

Frederick said I can't understand how you can take it like this but I'm in a worse position than you are. I've a suspended sentence.

Yes that's so said Karel.

Frederick said I envy you your composure you're marvelous and Karel looked at it and yes it was his composure.

Frederick said just think, I suppose Harold, Tony and the crowd are next door carousing at this moment. Karel admired Frederick's accent and enunciation. I'm going to lie down. Karel took off his coat and made a pillow of it.

They heard the voices in the others' cells: gob!... say any you got a cigarette... ohhh no butts here... what time is it?

That Frederick said is the way they always talk then they begin reminiscing like this: gee I'm in for stealing fifty dollars, it doesn't pay when I get out I'm not going to steal anything until I steal twenty thousand dollars.

Karel dozed off then he had to get up.   I can't sleep.

Frederick said isn't it terrible my mother I know she's having hysterics I wish I could telegraph her but there's no chance of that.   This'll call off my trip to Woodstock too O God.   He had started to whimper when he first got in the cell but Karel put out his hand on his.   It's very sportsmanlike of you he said you didn't run off, you stayed to save me.

Karel said uhm I could have got away easily. But somehow he couldn't be exactly sorry he didn't.   I'll write a poem.

How can you in such atmosphere?

In this or no other.   Isn't this a good first line. Karel recited it:

ripe is the urge, regular heart,

and going on:

asleep in the mind, flesh on the hand
picture and picture revolve into silence.

But he could compose no more and fell asleep' taking up most of the bench.

Frederick stayed awake until it was dawn.

Karel managed to sleep in three positions.   He would remember them he thought.

It's light Frederick said.   I wonder what time it is.

While waiting Karel wet his hair and put his

handkerchief smeared with mascara behind a pipe.

You still look like a queen Frederick said.

Bo Karel said and at that Frederick laughed.

They were let out of the cell and marched and Karel sat next to the sailor. The others included a gang of wops whatnot? who had come in later charged with assaulting one girl whatnot? (the impression they got was of concrete).

They had to wait after the ride, 8:30 Sunday morning, in one large cell at 57th Street station. The two who had trounced Manor got chummy and explained to Karel, looking up with their eyes and mouths to heaven in which there is God, that they both being Southern and drunk the night before had sought to displace without ceremony a negro from a seat in the subway and Manor had interfered and got his.

In the same cell there was one old thing by himself charged with rape. The girl in one difficult whole led up to a particularly red and particularly large bump under her left eye.

six months two weeks doin six aint that snap snap fucking dame are you the chauffeur

Karel and Frederick were not insulted once. They started to wean them from the cell. It was 9:30.

Karel leaned against the back of the bench. Frederick's lip was swollen; the bloodspots were still on his chin and on his glasses.

One officious person, a hundred percent bad

Irish Karel thought, came back just before they were called and cursed at Manor's assaulters who did not think that was a good sign and it wasn't for they went and got sixty days.

There was only now the sailor at one end of the bench and Frederick and Karel at the other. Suddenly Frederick said plaintively to him what did you do it for? The sailor smiled slightly. Now you see what a mess we're all in—all for nothing.

The sailor said, weakly, I don't know.

We didn't speak to you now did we? You'd better say that because it'll make it go better for all of us. Some one had said the ship'll give you five days on bread and water for this.

The sailor said well I don't know.

Then they called them. Karel and Frederick waited on a bench as straight as this: i i

They saw the detective who had finally appeared go up to the gob and whisper something.

Frederick turned to Karel and said now we *are* done for.

Karel looked somewhere and they were called. He got out his private band and to music they went in before justice and Karel handled his train very well he thought and there were not only two or three about four six people in the courtroom. Karel looked up at the magistrate after they had ranged them. The magistrate took one look. Karel imagined his switch was looking very well.

The magistrate said something but what did Karel care he had washed his gloves. The detective was sworn in first.

Frederick spoke up and said he would like an attorney beforehand. The magistrate who was white-haired, shrewd-humored, stooped, small-faced waved him aside and (Frederick said later) WINKED.

The detective told the truth except he said that the sailor had said they had said to the sailor: want to earn a few easy dollars?

When he said that Karel knew just what to do thinking the magistrate had his eye furtively upon him: he looked away with his teeth """ meaning what a lie. The magistrate must have seen him but Karel thought he did it with the right accent, modestly.

The magistrate looked at the sailor and said has the detective spoken the truth?

The sailor was dumb; in his own sweet soul he couldn't tell such a BIG LIE.

The magistrate smiled and looked at Karel intently and said your first name is Karel?

Yes.

And you don't live with your parents.

No.

Where do you live?

319 West Third Street.

And you say you are a free-lance writer, what do you mean by that, free of writing?

No Karel said taking a sidelong glance to see that his elegant train of feather dusters was in place, if it means anything I have appeared in the best places... the *Post*... the *Sun*...

Do you mean the magistrate asked that your articles have been accepted by these places?

Yes Karel said the *Bookman* as well... I have you see certain ambitions.

He cut him off DISCHARGED and Karel didn't have to lean forward to hear it.

Frederick started going toward the cells but someone pushed him into the aisle with Karel. The sailor was already there.

Then the magistrate leaned over and said sweetly but be more careful next time!

They went down some winding marble broad steps. The sailor walked in front of them.

Frederick was saying oh I can't believe it.

Karel said I knew it. I sensed it. There's at least one judge in the world with a civilized with a sense of civilization.

The sailor was walking down in front of them slowly.

Karel said I could kiss him right now.

They took the other side of the street and he did not look back at them.

They went to a drugstore and Karel had a chocolate ice-cream soda.

Frederick had a coca-cola with vanilla ice-cream in it.

CHAPTER FIFTEEN: SIEGE

KAREL thought about the pace at which things were walked through the heart without the breastbone being noticed. What had pounded on the closed door and what still was loitering was the clear spectre of either Louis or Gabriel, larger than life, but substantial as it had always been, giving the air its ruthless dirtiness. Louis had been to him a heart shaped like a bitter valentine, sworded and masked; he was like a mask from which imperative realities dangled.

Karel must squeeze his own heart into another shape, it had attracted wolves and burglars or for what had Louis come? It was the heart that held all houses. If he could give his heart to Louis, say take it and stab it and keep it, the door would have been opened again, but for fear it had stayed closed. Though the lace wavered the cupid wept. If some day it might burn up in an accidental fire, the remainder, the seared flakes, would lie there, complete, no heel would crush them, not Louis' nor another's, no wind would reach nor tear dissolve them.

He turned to Julian, crested with a sunlit comb. The sunlight hit Julian no matter where he was standing, and if he moved from the dark it was with a hello of closed lips. His lips were seen first and then the sunlight and then Julian. Julian had come and been and strangely he had ignored him, then had thought of him with pleasure. He still could not understand Julian's love for him as he did not know from what it derived, where it was or when it would come, as it did come sometimes, from nearer the sky than the earth. Where was its home, its house, its all-around heart—no door nor walls? Did he lie in it now or were they in it together? Karel asked God if the world floated or wheeled, or if they were in the grave, but looking at Julian from the side he knew they were not in the grave but that Louis and Gabriel were outside and perhaps not forever. Karel had always to be doing something either with his face or his brain so he would write a poem but he could not grasp the pencil tightly enough. He asked Julian do you think they're gone?

No Julian said they're there.

Karel's mind returned to the insistence of Louis' domain over him, the hypnotic way in which he had seized upon him as a mechanism to be controlled. Louis wanted him to deny everything but Louis. In that had seemed to lie Louis' economic salvation. Louis had been lover and beast. Karel started forward, has Louis actually had the temerity to believe that our affair could have existed in my imagination, only mine? Or that the idea of mutual chivalrousness could have been altogether eliminated as he had wished?

Louis had wanted, Karel saw plainly, to use him as Gabriel had used Louis. Through a compulsive worship, exercised by Gabriel, Louis had known love. Not animal love but some love —not Julian's love, something more potent and more of hate. He had wanted to redeem his humiliation through Karel's submission. The possibility of hate is all love needs to complete it Karel thought. Hatred and love at once raise love above earth. Louis hated but loved Gabriel. Gabriel, glowering, had seen Louis become apparently a master and master over Karel who would have worshipped Gabriel but for his lack of sexual attraction for him.

Karel thought of Gabriel's eyes, which could be accused of no crime; they were planets lighting an inner world: Gabriel is lost here, misshapen by his chances and by his achieving success with his chances, by his triumphs, for Gabriel cannot triumph, he is not made for greatness or for the definite gesture. He wants slaves but should be strong enough to do without them. Man may be rendered helpless by the idea of slaveholding and Gabriel has not thought enough of the idea. He has stood in the way of it, asking Louis for money and so Gabriel's enslavement to money has become apparent to Louis. But Louis had asked Karel for money and Karel had not been able to stand in the way for he had had no money.

You are free forever Karel called aloud suddenly. You are free now! Go!

Julian raised himself. Are you crazy? he asked.

I was telling them said Karel.

Tell them they're crazy said Julian.

You tell them that Karel said.

They know it Julian said lying down.

They both breathed hard and soft.

Then Karel said they are the secret of the night but so am I and so the siege is begun. No castles have fallen nor ladies been abducted for today we are too subtle for that. I'm going to the library.

Come back soon Julian said and was left alone.

Today is the day he said to himself when my bones seem to be aware of life, its fixability like its flexibility, its bottomless fears and its air of an exhausted hatefulness.

A spike was sticking in his left shoulder where he had a cold. I have been dull today but really my soul is freezing within me from ennui and pity. Louis and Gabriel are very like children; if I had sons I would train them up like them: debonair, destitute, devouring.

Today has done with me he continued when the pain in his shoulder was less but I have not done with today. Louis and Gabriel are nice, feedable youths, fencing with fate, fortunate or far from fortunate.

Time is a deception he thought, a monster which deceives. What looking kind of monster is it? It's a monster which looks and is looked at or completely looked at and completely non-looking, like the elephant. That is why today has been so fuzzy he announced excitedly to himself I have actually caught it looking at me out of its elephant-eye. He looked around to the door of the studio for someone was knocking.

With their minds they whipped the frozen streets of the last vestige of humanity.

Snow is good Gabriel said.

And ice Louis said.

Ice follows the wind and that's in your throat said Gabriel.

It's up your behind Louis said.

No Gabriel said it doesn't touch me.

Death will touch you.

He can touch me tomorrow Gabriel said.

He's a friend of mine Louis said. I asked him to keep away from me but gave him your address.

A child has no address.

An address is the important thing just now said Louis.

How about Julian's? asked Gabriel.

Find a weapon for him Louis said.

Find a weapon for him? Gabriel replied. I have found one.

I mean something he can understand.

I know what you mean said Gabriel.

At that moment they were in front of 319 West Third Street. Louis beat on the door and Julian saw them. He let them in.

How are you Julian? said Louis.

I'm all right said Julian looking ill-tempered. He was thinking about his typewriter. How are you?

Not so good said Louis. I mean Gabriel's not so good. He's got something to tell you.

Has he? Julian sat on the couch.

Gabriel was sitting there looking the other way. He turned his head around slowly and said you know Julian that I've got syphilis.

I heard something about it Julian said.

I've really got it Gabriel said but merely in my blood and I'm taking shots for it.

Louis was walking up and down, smoking and scowling.

I've been taking them for three months Gabriel said and looked seriously and piteously at Julian. I can't go on with them unless I have some money to give the doctor.

I'm sorry Julian said. I haven't any.

Furiously soft from Louis came goddamn and he went back to the street.

I really haven't Julian said sadly. I've got

forty dollars to live on until the sky drops more.

This is the way things are Gabriel said, brightening. The doctor has been treating me free for two months because he's had confidence in me. Now he's beginning to lose it. If the hypodermics stop at this stage all I've had will count for nothing. They *have* to go on for me to be cured. You believe me don't you?

Yes, I believe you.

If you go to the doctor and say here's ten dollars for Gabriel's treatments his faith in me will be *immediately* restored and I can have them for another couple of months. Otherwise I'll be —

Julian's resistance broke. He said you'd never pay me back the money.

But I would! Gabriel said. Louis is getting fifty dollars advance next week for a translation. I promise you'll have your ten back then. A thrill went through him which showed on his face. Today is the last day the doctor will wait. Here's his card. Take him the money and you'll see I'm not lying.

Julian put the card in his pocket and felt Gabriel's hand on his head. Louis is the boy for you he heard Gabriel say.

Is he? said Julian.

Yes said Gabriel taking his hand away and going towards the door. He turned with his hand on the latch and smiled and his features were a splintered mirror before it falls.

No sooner had he gone than Louis came back, repentant. I like you he said. He grabbed Julian who did not care and during one kiss Julian's teeth were clenched and his lips were together tight.

Louis departed as he had come, leaving Julian as he had found him.

Gabriel and Louis were struggling with each other. Louis said Gabriel and Gabriel said Louis as though‛ the names were familiar but precious objects, vaguely outlined in the darkness and to be knocked over at no price.

You can't get a five from him that way Gabriel said. For ten minutes he had been talking to a man in the hall next to a speakeasy; he had failed to get any money from him.

Will I get the whole five if I get it out of him? Louis asked. Neither had eaten for a day and a half.

Gabriel turned his dark blank eyes at him, his mouth a little dejected but firm. He said I know the man's psychology he wants to pity you. He helps weakness. He's not going to help ablebodied guys.

I'm not ablebodied protested Louis. I'll walk in and convince him I'm a consumptive by the way I stand!

Gabriel continued to express incredulous repose.

Stay here said Louis. Gabriel waited for his exit.

In five minutes Louis returned. He exclaimed shit. The dope is armored! he said. You've got to present a certificate from an institution for the sick.

Listen Louis you're all wrong, see? Wait a minute Gabriel said and flew into the doorway.

Louis waited, thinking of food and of Gabriel. Soon he saw Gabriel emerge and come toward him. As he came he waved to a taxi which drew up by the curb near Louis as Gabriel reached it.

Come on Gabriel called and got in. Louis followed him. Café Royal Gabriel said to the driver.

Louis leaned back and contemplated Gabriel. He did not doubt but that he had been successful. You got it? he said ecstatically.

Gabriel showed no corresponding ecstasy. A very little smile of satisfaction was beginning to appear on his lips, an expression Louis knew would burst into the sun of Italy.

Come on Gabriel have you got the five? Louis repeated.

Gabriel said for Christ's sake you don't think I went in for the five do you? I wouldn't rob Clapsaddle of his symbol of poverty. He hesitated. I got three bucks from Eddie.

From Eddie! Louis marvelled. Eddie was the bartender who had once thrown them out of the speakeasy.

Sure Gabriel said blandly I got it.

Before the miracle of money Louis' wonder at Gabriel's change of tactic melted. Clapsaddle had been the object; then it was Eddie. Strategy had been demonstrated that had not occurred to Louis.

They got out at the café and Gabriel paid the cab. Inside they ordered eggs and cigarettes and coffee. Gabriel got up and told Louis to stay there until he came back. Louis stayed thirty minutes and ordered more coffee. When Gabriel did not return Louis left his overcoat for the bill.

Harold, Frederick, Karel and Julian were walking down Fifth Avenue in some blue air colored with sunshine.

She had on sables worth at least fifteen thousand dollars Harold was saying. She was *charming*.

My mother said Frederick told me James Joyce was dead.

Dead! said Julian.

Yes she said he was dead. The man she said who looked like a grocer whose picture you had hanging over your desk.

But dead? said Karel.

Yes, she said he was sick for a long time.

I know said Karel.

They saw Louis in the same block coming their way.

The dear futile thing said Frederick.

Pass him by said Julian.

Karel felt a rose too big for him inside himself.

They meant to walk on but Louis stopped Julian and said say I've found a boy even prettier than you are.

I'd be so glad if the band would strike up now said Julian.

I want you to meet him Louis said. Upside-down he would spell money and that's what he's got.

Money's mammy too I suppose said Julian.

Let me see your teeth Louis said.

He showed him his teeth and Louis put a finger on Julian's upper lip and raised it.

What's the idea? Julian said.

Nothing said Louis. See you later.

Thank you desist! Frederick called.

And you can tell Gabriel if you see him Harold added not to ever come near my apartment again unless he wants to be arrested!

Louis laughed and walked away.

The four of them continued and Harold told about his going home and finding the door unlocked and inside Gabriel sitting on the bed smoking a cigarette.

Three suits of mine were missing Harold said and there he sat like Mother Goose saying he had just come by to pay me a call and found the door ajar. I was simply in a boil you can imagine my dear but what could I do? I wish now I had called an officer!

Why did Louis want to see my teeth Julian wondered.

You want to know why? Frederick said. He must have been kissing you! I saw him in Brentano's a few days ago and he had his gums and palate painted black. He's got trench-mouth, of course.

What would New York be without its tangible spectres Karel sighed. Louis is dirt mixed with diamond-dust.

Gabriel's blood is green with envy of eternity Harold said. Don't you think that's good Karel, Gabriel's blood is green with envy of eternity!

Can't you imagine all the lies and false impressions they give people Julian said.

Gabriel is eternity squirming Karel said and the color of Louis' blood is shitpurple.

They reached the studio and Harold unwrapped a painting of his he had been carrying, a gift for Karel and Julian. It was Eve with a monkey and snake.

Julian was looking at his gums in the mirror.

Where do you want this hung? Harold asked.

They decided to hang it over the downstairs couch.

Painting is always something of an anachronism Frederick said.

And literature Miss Spitzberger is only a form of guessing Harold retorted.

Karel, read this new poem of mine and tell me what you think of it said Frederick looking at Harold disdainfully.

Karel read it and said it has I think a suspension of attitude toward destiny which bespeaks inexperience.

Frederick raised his chin three more inches. Before he could think of a reply there was a tap on the window and a rattling of the lock.

Karel swayed towards the curtain, raised it and let it fall with horrified hands.

Who is it? said Julian.

I don't know and I don't want to know said Karel. Don't open the door.

Other raps were on the window louder and more insistent.

Julian looked out with no recognition and said what do you want?

I want to see youse a face said.

What about? Julian asked.

Let me in and I'll tell youse the face said.

You can tell me from where you are Julian said.

Open the door or I'll break the goddamned window!

Julian looked around at the others. Harold was holding his eyebrows up and two fingers to his cheek. Frederick looked like a bird the moment after it finds the sky nowhere. Karel forbade Julian to touch the lock.

Let's see what he wants said Julian. He postponed dread and pushed the door forward.

Who stepped in was unshaven and heavy. His cap didn't hide a scar near the eyebrow and he wanted to know which one was Julian.

I am said Julian.

Can I talk to youse privately he said. You needn't be afraid of me.

Come in here Julian said.

They went into the kitchenette.

Do you know two guys named Gabriel and Louis? he asked.

Julian said yes he knew them.

Have youse seen them lately?

Not recently Julian said.

Youse don't know where I could find them? No.

Well if youse see them again, tell them to look out for me because they're going to get it!

Julian wanted to know why.

What I'm going to do to them will be plenty, see. They told lies on me to the big boss!

They did? said Julian knowing nothing about the big boss.

Yeah. I'd seen the bastards around and the other day they asked me how much I'd take to clean out this place.

This place?

Yeah.   I said two hundred bucks.   That's the price.

And what did they say?

They didn't have the dough and I wouldn't do it for less so they goes and tells the boss a goddamned lie on me!

A dirty trick said Julian.   Come on out.

Listen to this he said to Karel.   He says that Gabriel and Louis tried to get him to clean this place out!

What? said Karel.   How?

That's the racket the man said.   Any joint in the Village stripped for two hundred bucks.   We drive up a truck, see.   My partner waits outside to warn the cops for me and I shoot the lock off if it needs it and take out everything whether you're home or not.

The others gasped.

It's nothing to me.   My partner and I get our share, the rest goes to the boss and that's all.

Have a cigarette Julian said and he took one and Julian lit it for him.

Relax babe the man said to Karel who was looking ill.   It's a business like any other.   I don't hold nothin against youse guys.   But when I see them two they're going to take a long ride.

Terror and sickness Julian murmured.

Karel heard him and said if you can find flowers more twin tell me.

But there is sex, a third flower, whose shadow, too, is death.

8

CHAPTER SIXTEEN : SHALL THE MOON DEVOUR THEM

KAREL felt again the sensations following Louis' baseness. It had been love with him and now it was impossible. Louis had said aloud, when he left: you beat me in the abstract. Perhaps, if circumstances had been different—but he could not tell. That was not the great cause of his resentment: Louis, the individual, was minor. How vicious he was as a factor in his life could not be determined, yet.

He turned the corner and saw a lurking figure which he recognized with God but not out loud. He walked to his door as Louis approached him. Karel turned to him and said what do you want?

I'd like to talk to you. Louis was smooth, unfrenzied.

What is there to say? Are you going to give me the things back?

That's what I wanted to talk to you about.

Why talk? Can't you bring them here? Louis, standing there, made no inaudible appeal to him.

No, that's the point. I can't talk here. I want to talk to you privately.

Did Louis imagine that he would permit him to make love to him now? Before Karel could answer Julian opened the door behind him.

How long are you going to stand out there?

Karel looked back to Louis. Wait a moment he said and went inside.

What does he want said Julian, his face saying it more vividly. He's been outside for twenty minutes, kicking on the door the first five of them.

He wants to return the things!

Well, let him bring them here. Julian moved a candle-stick from the chest of drawers to the table in the middle of the floor.

He wants to talk to me somewhere Karel said.

Julian swerved. Talk to you somewhere? Don't be a fool. You ought to call a policeman... or if we knew where to get ahold of the gangster.

Ssh! No! Karel's hands were counting their nerves. I'm going. I'll be back in an hour.

Julian would not look at him. Where is he taking you?

I don't know.

Well, neither do I.

I'm going to get the things back. Don't worry. He moved to the door. Good-bye.

Julian said good-bye and Karel was gone.

Louis started to leave.

Wait Karel said where are we going? It was beginning to sleet.

Come along for Christ's sake. Louis' impatience stimulated Karel's awareness. It's Gabriel's room—up here, he gestured with his head toward the east.

Oh. Karel got beside him and they walked quickly. They had not gone far before Gabriel appeared. He and Louis did not speak. Karel was conscious of the sleet, of the room ahead, of his manuscripts; of Louis, beautifully sinister.

Louis' key would not work. It was the wrong key. He went to the rear for the housekeeper.

Karel felt afraid. He almost turned and ran. In a moment Louis had come back. The housekeeper was not in. He tried the window which was ground floor front.

Is that the room? asked Karel.

Yes said Louis. He succeeded and walked through to admit Karel. He turned out the light in the small foyer which led off to other rooms and opened the door more widely for Karel to enter. It was an ordinary bedroom, for two. Having combed his hair at the bureau mirror, Karel sat on a chair close to the bed. Physical inequality had always been a factor in their relationship, at least after a certain point he thought.

Louis sat down on the bed, facing him. His face looked worn. It became set now. Take off the suit he said.

Karel looked gently at him. Why do you want me to do that?

I want the suit.

I didn't think you'd ever—Karel looked away.

The bleak bright electric light did not help him. Louis had pulled down the shade.

Hurry up—I don't want to wait!

Wait a minute said Karel. He did not intend to part with his suit if he could help it. He would have to wear Louis' poorly tailored one. He would have to face Julian, wearing it. Louis... I—his voice stopped.

Louis sneered. So you're being a woman. I'm not interested in your tears. Save them.

Karel felt sorry for himself now and a little sorry for Louis.

Listen said Louis. Do you think you can get away with threatening to call the cops on me? Say, I'm going to ruin you! I'm not going to let you alone. Take the suit off.

Louis—I—I don't want to, now. Wait a little.

Louis laughed. You're very cute. But I'm going to have that suit, and when I have the suit I won't be through.

You're as cruel as that?

Yes.

Louis... I haven't stopped loving you.

Stop that!

Louis, this is too much, I can't let you treat me like this... Tell me you don't want me to take the suit off. Think of what it would mean.

Listen Louis said you don't think you can pull that stuff now do you?

I'm not trying to pull anything. Do you think

I am? Aren't these tears real? Am I the sort of person to weep for nothing—for effect? He moved to a place beside Louis on the bed.

Say, you... Louis frowned viciously.

Karel looked away. Say that you don't mean what you said, that you really love me a little. He looked back, his cheeks tear-stained, at Louis.

Louis was gazing at him with sombreness and tight lips, strangely like and strangely unlike an animal. Do you mean that? he said.

I can't say why, but I still love you. I can't help it, that's all. Karel's hand went gently around Louis' shoulder. Do—you still love me? he said.

Louis kissed him furiously. The embrace swooped them together again.

In a few moments someone knocked and Karel went to the mirror and wiped his eyes.

Louis I want to speak to you Gabriel said through the door. Louis went out. Gabriel's voice penetrated the door. Listen do you think I want that guy here? He's got to get out!

Louis' expostulating tone was lower and Karel could not hear his replies.

In a moment he returned. Let's get out of here he said.

Karel adjusted his hat and put his manuscript book in the bag. What's the matter with him? he said.

Oh he's sore because we're together.

Karel started to ask another question but looked pretty instead.

Say, I need some money Louis said.

Karel extracted a quarter from his pocket. He handed it to Louis.

Quarters said Louis.

What do you expect? asked Karel.

Louis did not speak for several seconds. You don't care anything about me he said at last. You're pulling something all right.

Did Gabriel tell you that? Karel faced him.

I don't have to have Gabriel tell me anything. I wanted to see if you were sincere.

Do you mean the money?

No. I mean you haven't asked me where I'm staying, how I'm fixed.

What do you expect me—

Say, if you love me you'll find a place for me to stay tonight.

What? Aren't you staying here with Gabriel?

No—and I don't want to stay with him now.

What can I do? asked Karel.

What can you do? I guess you think you can treat me like this? The wild, suppressed whine entered his voice.

Like what?

If you loved me you'd be willing to leave Julian, you'd see that I didn't starve... You're a harlot!

Louis, I tell you I'm going to help you.

I think that's a lie Louis said. I think you're never going to help me again. I think I want that suit.

When—now? What do you mean?

Right now!

Don't be silly—

Louis stepped up closely to him and clutched one of his lapels. Who do you think you are?

Karel's lips pouted and quivered. He did not resist having his topcoat taken off, then his jacket, then his vest and, lastly, falling over on the bed, his trousers. Louis leaned over and Karel saw him kissing him before he felt the bite. Then Karel screamed.

THE END

———

IMPRIMERIE VENDOME
338, Rue Saint-Honoré
——— Paris ———

HOMOSEXUALITY

Lesbians and Gay Men
in Society, History and Literature

Acosta, Mercedes de. **Here Lies The Heart.** 1960

Bannon, Ann. **I Am a Woman.** 1959

Bannon, Ann. **Journey To a Woman.** 1960

Bannon, Ann. **Odd Girl Out.** 1957

Bannon, Ann. **Women in The Shadows.** 1959

Barney, Natalie Clifford. **Aventures de L'Esprit.** 1929

Barney, Natalie Clifford. **Traits et Portraits.** 1963

Brooks, Romaine. **Portraits, Tableaux, Dessins.** 1952

Carpenter, Edward. **Intermediate Types Among Primitive Folk.** 1919

Casal, Mary. **The Stone Wall.** 1930

Cory, Donald Webster. **The Homosexual in America.** 1951

Craigin, Elisabeth. **Either Is Love.** 1937

Daughters of Bilitis. **The Ladder.** Volumes I - XVI. Including an **Index To The Ladder** by Gene Damon. 1956 - 1972. Nine vols.

Documents of the Homosexual Rights Movement in Germany, 1836 - 1927. 1975

Ellis, Havelock and John Addington Symonds. **Sexual Inversion.** 1897

Fitzroy, A. T. **Despised and Rejected.** 1917

Ford, Charles and Parker Tyler. **The Young and Evil.** 1933

Frederics, Diana. **Diana: A Strange Autobiography.** 1939

Friedlaender, Benedict. **Renaissance des Eros Uranios.** 1904

A Gay Bibliography. 1975

A Gay News Chronology, 1969 - May, 1975. 1975

Gordon, Mary. **Chase of the Wild Goose.** 1936

Government Versus Homosexuals. 1975

Grosskurth, Phyllis. **John Addington Symonds.** 1964

Gunn, Peter. **Vernon Lee: Violet Paget, 1856 - 1935.** 1964

A Homosexual Emancipation Miscellany, c. 1835 - 1952. 1975

Karsch-Haack, F[erdinand]. **Das Gleichgeschlechtliche Leben der Naturvölker.** 1911

Katz, Jonathan. **Coming Out!** 1975

Lesbianism and Feminism in Germany, 1895 - 1910. 1975

Lind, Earl. **Autobiography of an Androgyne.** 1918

Lind, Earl. **The Female-Impersonators.** 1922

Loeffler, Donald L. **An Analysis of the Treatment of the Homosexual Character in Dramas Produced in the New York Theatre From 1950 to 1968.** 1975

Mallet, Françoise. **The Illusionist.** 1952

Miss Marianne Woods and Miss Jane Pirie Against Dame Helen Cumming Gordon. 1811 - 1819

Mattachine Society. **Mattachine Review.** Volumes I - XIII. 1955 - 1966. Six vols.

Mayne, Xavier. **Imre: A Memorandum.** 1908

Mayne, Xavier. **The Intersexes.** 1908

Morgan, Claire. **The Price of Salt.** 1952

Niles, Blair. **Strange Brother.** 1931

Olivia. **Olivia.** 1949

Rule, Jane. **The Desert of the Heart.** 1964

Sagarin, Edward. **Structure and Ideology in an Association of Deviants.** 1975

Steakley, James D. **The Homosexual Emancipation Movement in Germany.** 1975

Sturgeon, Mary C. **Michael Field.** 1921

Sutherland, Alistair and Patrick Anderson. **Eros: An Anthology of Friendship.** 1961

Sweet, Roxanna Thayer. **Political and Social Action in Homophile Organizations.** 1975

Tobin, Kay and Randy Wicker. **The Gay Crusaders.** 1972

Ulrichs, Carl Heinrich. **Forschungen Über Das Rätsel Der Mannmännlichen Liebe.** 1898

Underwood, Reginald. **Bachelor's Hall.** 1937

[Vincenzo], Una, Lady Troubridge. **The Life of Radclyffe Hall.** 1963

Vivien, Renée **Poèmes de Renée Vivien.** Two vols. in one. 1923/24

Weirauch, Anna Elisabet. **The Outcast.** 1933

Weirauch, Anna Elisabet. **The Scorpion.** 1932

Wilhelm, Gale. **Torchlight to Valhalla.** 1938

Wilhelm, Gale. **We Too Are Drifting.** 1935

Winsloe, Christa. **The Child Manuela.** 1933